THE BEASTS OF CLAWSTONE CASTLE

EVA IBBOTSON

MACMILLAN CHILDREN'S BOOKS

First published 2005 by Macmillan Children's Books

This edition published 2014 by Macmillan Children's Books
an imprint of Pan Macmillan
a division of Macmillan Publishers Limited
20 New Wharf Road, London N1 9RR
Associated companies throughout the world
www.panmacmillan.com

ISBN 978-1-4472-6563-4

1 3 5 7 9 8 6 4 2

A CIP catalogue record for this book is available from
the British Library.

Typeset by Intype Libra Ltd
Printed and bound by CPI Group (UK) Ltd, Croydon CR0 4YY

BEASTS OF CLAWSTONE CASTLE

E   bbotson was born in Vienna, but when
th   Nazis came to power her family fled to
En   nd and she was sent to boarding school.
She ecame a writer while bringing up her
fo   children, and her bestselling novels
ha   been published around the world. Her
boc s have also won and been shortlisted for
ma   prizes. *Journey to the River Sea* won the
Ne   é Gold Award and was runner-up for
the Whitbread Children's Book of the Year
and the Guardian Children's Fiction Prize.
The Star of Kazan won the Nestlé Silver Award
and was shortlisted for the Carnegie Medal.
The Secret of Platform 13 was shortlisted for the
Smarties Prize, and *Which Witch?* was runner-
up fo he Carnegie Medal. *The Ogre of Oglefort*
was shortlisted for the Guardian Children's
Fiction Prize and the Roald Dahl Funny Prize.
Eva Ibbotson died peacefully in October 2010
at the age of eighty-five.

Books by Eva Ibbotson

The Beasts of Clawstone Castle
Dial A Ghost
The Great Ghost Rescue
The Haunting of Hiram
Monster Mission
Not Just a Witch
The Ogre of Oglefort
The Secret of Platform 13
Which Witch?

Let Sleeping Sea-Monsters Lie . . .
and Other Cautionary Tales

The Dragonfly Pool
Journey to the River Sea
The Star of Kazan

For older readers
A Company of Swans
Magic Flutes
The Morning Gift
The Secret Countess
A Song for Summer

To the children of Rock Hall School

One

There are children whose best friends have two legs, and there are children whose best friends have four – or a thousand, or none at all.

Madlyn was very fond of *people*. Ordinary, two legged people. She liked the girls at her school and in her dancing class, and she liked the people she met at the swimming pool and in the supermarket and the library. When you like people they usually like you back, and Madlyn had so many invitations to parties and sleepovers that if she had accepted them all she would never have had a night at home. She was very pretty, with silky fair hair and clear blue eyes and a deep laugh – the kind that infects other people and makes them think that being alive is a thoroughly good idea.

Rollo, her brother, who was two years younger, was quite different. He did not mind people, but his truest friends lived under stones or in the rafters of the local church or in heaps of earth in the park, and if he was writing a birthday card it was more likely to be addressed to his stump-tailed skink than to a boy in his class.

The skink didn't exactly belong to him – it lived in London Zoo – but he had adopted it. The zoo runs a very good scheme whereby children can choose an animal to adopt and when he was six years old his

1

parents had taken him to the zoo to choose something he liked.

The cuddly animals like the wombats and bush-babies and fluffy possums all had waiting lists of children wanting to adopt them, but Rollo had always liked lizards and as soon as he met Stumpy's eyes and saw his berry-blue tongue flicker out he knew the creature was for him.

The children lived in a ground-floor flat in a pleasant part of south London. Their parents were funny and clever and nice, but they were apt to be a little bit frantic because of their jobs. Mrs Hamilton ran an experimental theatre which put on interesting plays but kept on running out of money, and Mr Hamilton was a designer and had to have good ideas about what people should do with their houses.

Both of them worked long hours and never knew when they were going to be home and, when Rollo was a baby and Madlyn had just started school, life had been rather a muddle. But as Madlyn grew older everything became easier. Though she loved parties and clothes and going out with her friends, she was a sensible and practical girl and soon she began to take a hand in the running of her home. She left notes for her mother, reminding her to pick up Rollo's coat from the cleaners and make an appointment with the dentist; she rang her father at the office and told his secretary that a man from Hong Kong had come to see him and was eating doughnuts in the kitchen. And almost every morning she found the car keys, which her parents had lost.

Most of all, she saw to it that Rollo had what he

needed, which was not always the same as what other boys needed. She soothed him when stupid people asked after his skunk instead of his skink; she stopped the cleaning lady from throwing away the snails he kept in a jar under his bed, and when he had a nightmare she was beside him almost as soon as he woke. It wasn't that she loved him – she did, of course – but it was more than that. It was as though she was able to get right inside his skin. As for Rollo, when he came in through the front door he looked first of all for Madlyn and if she was there he gave a little sigh of content and went off to his room to get on with his life.

When everything is going along normally it is hard to imagine why there should be a change. But at the beginning of the summer term when Madlyn was eleven an offer came from an American college inviting Mr Hamilton to spend two months in New York setting up a course for people who wanted to start their own design business. There was a room in the college for him and his wife, but nothing at all was said about the children.

'We can't possibly leave them,' said Mr Hamilton.

'And we can't possibly take them along,' said Mrs Hamilton.

'So we'll have to refuse.'

'Yes.' But the Americans had offered a lot of money and the car was making terrible noises and bills were dropping through the letter box in droves.

'Unless we send them to the country. They ought to be in the country,' said Mrs Hamilton. 'It's where children ought to be.'

'But where?' asked her husband. 'Where in the

country? Where would we send them for two whole months?'

'Up to the Scottish border. To Clawstone. To Uncle George at Clawstone Castle. I've always meant to take them there but . . .'

By 'but' she meant that Uncle George lived in the bleakest and coldest part of England and was a thoroughly grumpy old man.

'We'll see what Madlyn thinks,' said her father.

Madlyn, when they put it to her, knew exactly what she thought. She thought, *no*. She had four parties to go to, the school was planning a visit to the ballet and she had been chosen to play Alice in the end-of-term production of *Alice in Wonderland*. What's more, from what she had overheard, she was sure that Uncle George's castle was not the kind that appeared in cartoon films, with gleaming towers and princes, but the other kind – the kind one learned about in History lessons, with things like mottes and baileys and probably rats.

'It would mean wearing wellington boots all day,' she said, 'and I haven't got any.' Rollo was lying on the floor, drawing a picture of a Malayan tapir which lived near his skink in the zoo. Now he looked up and said, 'I have. I've got wellington boots.'

Mr and Mrs Hamilton said nothing. The Americans were offering enough money to enable them to fix the car and pay every single bill in the house when they got back. All the same, they stayed silent.

The silence was a long one.

But Madlyn was a good person, the kind that wanted other people to be happy. Being good like that is bad luck, but there is nothing to be done.

'Oh, all right,' said Madlyn at last. 'But I want proper boots, green ones, and a real oilskin and sou'wester, and an Aran knit sweater, and an electric torch with three different colours . . .'

She was a person who could always be cheered up by a serious bout of shopping.

Two

Sir George always woke early on Saturday morning because that was when the castle was open to the public and there was a lot to do.

He lifted his creaking legs out of the four-poster bed, which was propped up at one end with a wooden fish crate to stop it falling down, and padded off to the bathroom. There was no hot water but he was used to that; the boiler was almost as old as Sir George himself and Clawstone was not a place for people who wanted to be comfortable.

It did not take him long to get ready. His hair was so sparse that brushing it was dangerous, so he only passed a comb lightly through what was left of it and put on his long woollen underpants and the mustard-coloured tweed suit he wore summer and winter. But today, because it was Open Day, he also put on a tie. It was a regimental tie because he had served all through the war in the army and got a leg wound which still made him limp.

'Right! Time to get going,' he said to himself – and went over to the mantelpiece to fetch the bunch of keys which lived in a box underneath a painting of a large white bull. Once Sir George's bedroom walls had been covered in valuable paintings, but they had all been sold and only the bull was left. Then he went downstairs to unlock the door of the museum and the dungeon and the armoury, so that the visitors tramping through the castle got their money's worth.

Sir George's sister, Miss Emily, also woke early on Open Day, and wound her thin grey plait of hair more carefully round her head than usual. Then she put on the long brown woollen skirt which she had knitted herself. During the many years she had worn it, it had taken on the outlines of her behind, but not at all unpleasantly because she was a thin lady and her behind was small. Today, though, because it was Open Day, she also knotted a scarf round her throat. It was one of those weak-looking chiffon scarves which look as though they need feeding up, but Emily was fond of it. She had found it under a sofa cushion when she went to move a nest of field mice who had decided to breed there, and the slightly mousy smell which clung to it did not trouble her in the least.

Then she fetched her keys, which also lived on the mantelpiece, but not under a painting of a bull – under a painting of a cow. Like her brother George, Emily had once slept in a room full of costly paintings, but now only the cow was left.

The third member of the family never came out of his room on Open Day. This was Howard Percival, a cousin of Sir George's and Miss Emily's. He was a middle-aged man with a grey moustache and so shy that if he saw a human being he had not known for at least twenty years he hurried away down the corridors and shut himself up in his room.

Emily always hoped that Howard would decide to help; there were so many things he could have done to interest the visitors, but she knew it was no good asking him. When shyness gets really bad it is like an illness, so she just knocked on his door to tell him that the day had begun and went downstairs to the kitchen where she found Mrs Grove, who came in from the village to help, preparing breakfast.

'Nothing doing with Mr Howard, then?' she asked, and Emily sighed and shook her head.

'His door's bolted.'

A frown spread over Mrs Grove's kind, round face. It was her opinion that Sir George and Miss Emily should have been stricter with their cousin. With everyone working so hard for Open Day he could have pulled his weight. But all she said was, 'I'll put the coffee on.'

Emily nodded and went through to the storeroom to look at the treasures she had made for the gift shop.

People who pay to look round castles and stately homes usually like to have something to buy, and Emily had done her best. She had made three lavender bags, which she had sewn out of muslin – the kind that is used for bandages – and filled with flower heads from the bushes in the garden. One of them leaked a little but the other two were intact, and since so far no one had actually bought any bags there would probably be enough for today. She had prepared two bowls of dried rose petals, which were meant to scent people's rooms: pot-pourri, it was called. The trouble was that it was difficult to dry anything properly in the castle, which was always damp, both inside and out, so the petals had gone mouldy underneath. Now she packed the scones she had baked into plastic bags and stuck little labels on them saying 'Baked in the Clawstone Bakery', which was perfectly true. She had baked them herself the day before on the ancient stove in the kitchen and they were not really burnt. A little dark round the edges perhaps but not actually *burnt*.

It was important not to lose heart; Emily knew that, but just for a moment she felt very sad and discouraged. She worked so hard, but she knew that never in a hundred years would her gift shop catch up with the gift shop at Trembellow Towers. The gift shop at Trembellow was larger. It had table mats stamped with the Trembellow coat of arms. It had furry animals bought in from Harrods and books of poems about Nature and embroidered tea towels. And leading out of the gift shop at Trembellow was a tea room with proper waitresses and soft music playing.

No wonder people turned left at the Brampeth Crossroads and made their way to Trembellow instead of Clawstone. And it seemed so unfair, because the people who owned Trembellow did not *need* money; they only *wanted* it, which is not the same at all.

But she would catch up, Emily told herself; she would not give in to despair. She was always having good ideas. Only yesterday she had found some old balls of wool left in a disused linen bag which would knit up into mittens and gloves. The moths had been at some of them but there were plenty left.

Sir George, meanwhile, was opening up the rooms he had prepared to make things interesting for the visitors. He was a private sort of person and found it difficult to have people tramping through his house and making loud remarks, which were often rather rude, but once he had decided it had to be done, he worked hard to see that the people who came got value for their money.

So he had filled the billiard room with all sorts of

things – his grandmother's old sewing machine and a rocking horse with a broken leg and a box of stones he had found on the beach when he was a boy, and he had put a big notice on the door saying 'Museum'.

Down in the cellar he had collected ancient contraptions which might well have been used as torture instruments – rusty mangles which pulled at the laundry maids' arms as they turned the handle, and huge washtubs which they might have drowned in, and dangerous boilers which had to be heated with fires underneath that could easily have burned them to death. He had labelled the door 'Dungeon', and he had made an armoury too, into which he had put his rifle from the war and the bow and arrow he had had as a little boy and various pikes and halberds and axes he had found lying about.

But he too, as he tidied the exhibits and straightened the signs saying 'Danger' on those floorboards which had gone rotten, had to be careful not to feel discouraged and sad. For he knew that for every car which made its way to Clawstone, there would be ten cars at least going to Trembellow. And really he couldn't wonder at it. Trembellow had a proper dungeon with throat manacles and racks on which people had been stretched and died in agony. Trembellow's museum housed priceless rings; the weapons in the armoury had belonged to Charles the First. And the man who owned Trembellow was as rich as Sir George was poor.

At ten o'clock Mrs Grove's sister Sheila came to take the tickets, bringing with her a duffel bag filled with things that people in the village had sent for the museum and the shop. The postmistress had had a clear-out in her attic and found the old cardboard gasmask case which had held her grandfather's gas mask in the war. And Mr Jones had made a new puzzle for the shop.

Mr Jones was the retired sexton and had taken up fretwork. He made jigsaw puzzles by sticking pictures on to plywood and sawing them into wiggly shapes, and he was very kind about letting Miss Emily have them to sell in the gift shop. The one he had sent this morning was a picture of two vegetable marrows and a pumpkin which he had managed to saw into no less than twenty-seven pieces.

Then Mrs Grove and her sister set up the folding table and brought out the roll of tickets and the saucer for the change and laid out the pamphlets Sir George had written giving the history of the castle, and Open Day began.

It did not go well. By lunchtime only ten people had come and there had been some unpleasantness because Emily had left her bedroom door open and a family with two small boys had gone in and peered at her nightdress, which they thought had been worn by Queen Victoria and was part of the tour. Nobody bought a lavender bag and a man with a red face brought back the jigsaw puzzle he had bought the week before and asked for his money to be returned because the pieces did not fit properly. It was not until the visitors had made their way out of the castle and were wandering about in the gardens that Sir George and his sister could relax.

But today their quiet time did not last for long because the postman brought a most distressing letter.

It was from Sir George's niece, Patricia Hamilton, asking if they could have Madlyn and Rollo to stay for two months in the summer.

The parents apologized; they hated to ask favours, but if it was possible it would be a wonderful thing for the children.

'Children!' said Sir George, leaning back in his chair. His voice was grim. He might as well have been saying 'Smallpox!' or 'Shipwreck!'

'Oh dear, children,' repeated Emily. 'I do find children a little alarming. Especially if they are small.'

'Children are generally small,' said Sir George crabbily. 'Otherwise they would not be children.'

Emily was about to say that actually some children were quite large these days because they ate the wrong things – she had read about it in the paper – but she didn't.

'Do you think they will shout and scream and . . . play practical jokes?' she asked nervously. 'You know . . . string across the stairs and apple-pie beds?'

Sir George was frowning, staring out of the window at the park.

'If they let off fireworks and frighten the animals I shall have to beat them,' he said.

But the thought of beating children was seriously alarming. You had to catch them first, and then upend them. . . and his joints were a trouble to him even when he had to get up from his chair. What if they were the kind of children who *squirmed*?

'They have been brought up in town,' he went on disapprovingly. 'The boy will probably pretend to be a motor car and make those vroom-vroom noises all the time.'

'And the girl will wear thin shoes and carry a handbag.'

A gloomy silence fell. Then:

'Cousin Howard won't like it,' said Emily.

'No,' said her brother, 'Cousin Howard won't like it at all. But the children are "family". Patricia is my niece. They have Percival blood.'

Emily nodded. Blood is blood and cannot be argued with – and the next day they wrote to say that of course Madlyn and Rollo would be welcome to spend the summer at Clawstone.

Three

Madlyn stood still in the centre of the courtyard and looked round at the towers and the battlements which surrounded her.

'Poor thing,' she said.

'Poor thing' is not usually what people say to castles, but Madlyn was right. Clawstone did not look well. There were blobs of lichen – green blobs and yellow blobs and purple blobs – all over the steps which led to the front entrance. The statue of a knight-at-arms had lost his nose, the two cannons which flanked the doorway were covered in rust.

And the two old people who came carefully down the steps to greet them looked rather like poor things also. Sir George had bent down, ready to shake hands, but it did not seem certain that he would be able to straighten himself up again. Emily's skirt was coming unravelled at the hem, and her watery eyes were worried.

The children had travelled in charge of Rollo's former childminder, a plump and caring lady called Katya. She loved the children and she loved England, but she did not care for the English language, which she spoke oddly or not at all.

'Is here Madlyn, is here Rollo,' she said. Then thumping herself on the chest: 'Is here Katya.'

Uncle George shook hands with everybody. Now

14

that they were here he had to admit that the children did not look dangerous. Madlyn was very pretty and Rollo was very small and the lady who had brought them was returning to London on the following day.

As the children followed Aunt Emily up the stone staircase and down the corridor which led to their rooms a figure in a long dressing gown appeared suddenly and came towards them. They stopped, ready to greet him, but when he saw them the man turned round abruptly and scuttled away.

'Oh dear,' said Aunt Emily when he was out of sight. 'I did so hope he would say good evening to you. He's a very polite person really, but so dreadfully shy.'

'Who is he?' asked Madlyn.

'It's Cousin Howard. He finds it so hard to meet new people but I hoped as you were "family" . . . Never mind, I'm sure when he knows you better . . . Now here are your rooms.'

Their rooms were in the newest part of the castle, which was only three hundred years old. They were next to each other with a connecting door between them, and Katya's room was across the corridor, so they slept well and were up early next morning to explore.

They found Aunt Emily in the kitchen with Mrs Grove, who always came in early from the village. Madlyn liked Mrs Grove straight away; she was sensible and friendly, and when Rollo said he didn't like porridge, that was the end of that. She didn't try to persuade him or fuss and when Madlyn explained that he had toast fingers and Marmite for breakfast

15

every day of his life, she said that was perfectly normal.

'Ned used to eat peanut butter day in and day out when he was small, and he's strong enough now.'

'Who's Ned?' asked Madlyn.

'My son. He's around somewhere; he comes to give me a hand when he isn't at school.'

'How old is he?' Madlyn wanted to know.

'He's eleven.'

After breakfast they said goodbye to Katya, who left for the station in a taxi, and then they set off to explore the castle, which they found very interesting, though rather cold and damp.

Madlyn particularly liked the museum. It wasn't much like the museums in London but it was very . . . personal. In the London museums you never saw rocking horses with missing legs or stuffed ducks that had choked on a stickleback or dog collars which had belonged to Jack Russell terriers who were able to climb trees. There was a set of brushes for cleaning out Northumbrian Small Pipes and a round, brownish thing covered in some kind of skin, which was labelled 'The Clawstone Hoggart'. It was on a table all by itself and was obviously important, but they had no idea what it was.

Rollo of course liked the dungeon. He could see at once that all the old machines that had been used for doing the washing could easily have been instruments of torture – and in a corner behind the mangle he found two fat cockroaches whose chestnut wing cases shone most beautifully in the dusk.

But when they had explored all the rooms that they

16

could get into they came back to Mrs Grove in the kitchen.

'I can't find the television set,' said Madlyn.

'There isn't one, dear. Sir George doesn't want one in the place. Nor no computer either.'

Madlyn tried to take this in. She had never been in a house without a television.

'It's my favourite programme tomorrow afternoon,' she said. 'And Rollo always has his animal programmes.'

'You can come and watch in my house,' said Mrs Grove. 'The village is only five minutes down the road. Ned'll show you.'

Madlyn thanked her and made her way to Aunt Emily's room. She could hear someone hoovering on an upstairs landing but when she got closer the hoovering stopped and when she went to investigate there was nobody there.

The idea had been that Aunt Emily would look after Madlyn and her brother with Mrs Grove helping out when necessary, but it soon became clear that it was going to be the other way round.

As far as Madlyn could see, it was Aunt Emily who needed help, and she needed it badly.

She needed help with her hair, which looked like a grey worm that had landed by mistake on her head and passed on to a better world; she needed help with her clothes, which she had lost track of in various drawers – and she certainly needed help with the things she was knitting for the gift shop.

Aunt Emily was very fond of knitting, but unfortunately you can be fond of something and not be very good at it, and Madlyn was not surprised that the gloves and scarves she had made were not selling well. After all, most people have five fingers; there is really nothing to be done about that.

'What about crochet, Aunt Emily?' suggested Madlyn. 'We could make table-mats and doilies; they're easy – they just go round and round.' Aunt Emily thought this was a good idea, and she showed Madlyn the patchwork tea cosy she was working on.

'Do you think people would notice if I used snippets from George's pyjamas? I mean, pyjamas aren't really . . . underwear . . . are they?' said Emily. 'It's not as though they were *striped*. Or flannel. Striped flannel would never do, I see that.'

In the next few days Madlyn was busier than she could remember, and she was glad of it because she missed her parents more than she could have imagined. She mended the leaking lavender bags, she turned the pot-pourri to stop it mouldering, she helped Mrs Grove to make fudge to sell the visitors in fancy bags. When Sir George found out how neat her handwriting was he asked her to help with the labels in the museum. She was even allowed to make a new label for the Clawstone Hoggart.

'What exactly *is* a Hoggart, Uncle George,' the children had asked at lunch when they first came.

'A Hoggart?' Uncle George had looked vague.

'Yes. The Clawstone Hoggart in the museum. We've never seen one before.'

'No . . . well . . .' Sir George took a sip of water. 'We think it might be . . .' He turned to his sister. 'You tell them.'

'We found it in an old chest,' said Emily. 'It just said

"Hoggart" – and of course it was found here so it is a "Clawstone Hoggart". But we're not sure exactly . . . Cousin Howard is looking into it.'

If Cousin Howard was trying to find out what a Hoggart was, that was all that he was doing. He still hurried away from the children; he didn't come down to meals; he never spoke. His room and his library seemed to be the whole of his world.

Rollo was also helping, but in his own way. He had found places in the gardens and grounds where if you sat quietly things came and looked at you. Red squirrels and voles and sometimes a vixen with her cubs. There was a badger's sett by the stream and under the stones in the shrubbery a whole fascinating world of beetles and centipedes as fierce as they were tiny.

What he liked particularly about Clawstone was that there wasn't much difference between the outside and the inside of the castle. In London you had to go out of doors to see animals, but here there were mice in the sofa cushions and owl pellets in the attics and hedgehogs in the scullery clanking about and looking for their saucers of milk. And though he knew that animals were best left where they were, Rollo made an exhibit for the museum which he thought would interest the visitors. It was a shoebox stuffed with poplar twigs in which hawk-moth caterpillars crawled about, chomping the leaves.

The children had arrived on a Monday and, though the next Open Day was not until the following Saturday, Madlyn could see how hard everyone was preparing for it. It wasn't just the lavender bags and the scones; the rooms had to be cleaned and the notices

19

put up and the car park checked for potholes and the cobwebs swept out of the toilets. Uncle George and Aunt Emily did a lot of this, but they would have been lost without Mrs Grove.

And Mrs Grove had an unpaid helper. She had Ned.

Madlyn had heard the sound of someone hoovering often in the first days, but when she went to investigate the noise stopped and there was no one to be seen.

She put up with this as long as she could. Then on the third day she decided she had had enough.

'I know you're there,' she yelled from the bottom of the stairs, 'and I think you're rude and horrible and unfriendly to keep hiding.'

For a while the noise of the machine went on. Then it stopped and a boy came down the stairs towards her. He had very blue eyes and bright ginger hair, and Madlyn knew at once that it was going to be all right, that she had found a friend. All the same, she decided to be offended for a little longer.

'Hiding from people is hurtful,' she said sternly. Ned came down the last of the steps till he was level with her.

'I didn't know what you were going to be like. You could have been like the Honourable Olive.'

'Who's the Honourable Olive?'

'She's an awful girl. Horrible. She lives at Trembellow and she looks like a pickle, all sour and vinegary – but snobby with it.'

'Well, I'm not snobby and I'm not a pickle.'

'No,' said Ned. He had never seen a less pickled looking girl.

'Why is she the Honourable Olive?'

'Her father's a lord. He didn't used to be – he used to be just an ordinary bloke, but he made all those traffic cones they have on motorways to tell people they can't go there. He made millions of them and he got very rich and they made him a lord and he bought Trembellow Towers.'

'Yes, I see.'

Even in the few days she had been at Clawstone, Madlyn had heard about Trembellow Towers.

'You could come to my house this afternoon if you like,' said Ned. 'There's a programme about whales for your brother. And you could email your parents if you wanted to.'

Madlyn's face lit up. If there was one thing she wanted more than any other it was to make contact with her parents, and she knew that she'd been right about Ned. He was going to be a true and proper friend.

The children felt at home straight away in Mrs Grove's bungalow. It was a small modern house, with just three rooms and a tiny garden, and it was marvellously warm and clean and comfortable. The TV chuntered away to itself quietly in the corner, there were geraniums on the window sill and from the kitchen came the smell of unburned scones and flapjacks baking in the oven.

Mrs Grove's husband had been killed two years earlier, when a drunken lout in a Jaguar had run into his delivery van, but if she was sad she kept the sadness inside – and she still had Ned.

While Rollo settled himself down in front of the whales, Ned took Madlyn off to his room and sent a message to New York, and they were lucky: by the time they had finished tea there was a reply saying all was well.

When they got back to the castle they found Aunt Emily riddling the kitchen range. There was a smudge of soot on her nose and her hair was coming down.

'Isn't it the dearest little house?' she said wistfully when they told her about their afternoon. 'I've always wanted to live in a house like that. No stairs and you just turn a knob and the fire comes on.'

'Well, couldn't you, Aunt Emily?' asked Madlyn. 'Do you have to go on living here?'

Aunt Emily sighed. 'I'm afraid we do,' she said. She rubbed her nose, spreading the soot a little further.

'One has to do one's duty.'

There were now only two more days to Open Day. Mr Jones in the village had sent another jigsaw puzzle; it was a picture of a town councillor on a platform making a speech. Aunt Emily stayed up till midnight finishing the tea cosy, and Madlyn sprayed fresh disinfectant into the toilets and arranged a posy of wild flowers to put on the table in the entrance hall.

But on the morning of the actual day, Sir George came down from the battlements holding his telescope and looking grim.

'Cars streaming off to Trembellow,' he said. 'Dozens of them. Hardly a one coming this way.'

Sir George was right. By eleven o'clock only four people had bought tickets and made their way up the front steps of the castle.

Madlyn was sitting beside Mrs Grove at the table where the tickets were sold, ready to help with giving change and handing out booklets. She had taken over from Mrs Grove's sister who now had a morning job in the village shop.

Now, as the big clock in the courtyard ticked up the minutes, she turned to her and said, 'Mrs Grove, why does it matter so much that people come to the castle? Couldn't Uncle George sell it and he and Aunt Emily go and live in a bungalow? Then they wouldn't need nearly so much money for themselves.'

Mrs Grove turned to her. 'Why, bless you, it isn't the castle they want the money for and it isn't for themselves. I've never met two people who spent less.'

'Well, what then? What do they have to have the money for? Why is the money so important?'

Mrs Grove patted her hand. 'I thought you knew. It's for the cows. It's the cows they need it for. Everything at Clawstone is for the cows.'

Four

It was not till the following day that Madlyn really understood what Mrs Grove had told her, because that was the day when she and Rollo were driven through the gates of Clawstone Park.

They went in Sir George's ancient Land Rover and, as he stopped to take out a large iron key and unlock the padlock, it seemed to Madlyn that a change came over her great-uncle. He seemed to become taller and more upright, less stooped and weary-looking, as if he knew that what he was to show them could be equalled nowhere in the world.

They moved forward, and as the gates in the high stone wall closed again behind them they seemed to be entering a kind of Paradise. It was silent except for the calling of the curlews on the hill; the trees standing in full-leaved clumps looked as though they had stood there since the beginning of time; the stream beside which they drove was as clear and clean as rivers must have been in the Garden of Eden. No artificial sprays or chemicals were allowed inside the park, so that the grassy banks were studded with wild flowers, and the blossom on the gorse bushes dazzled with their gold.

They bumped their way across the fields, and crossed a shallow ford.

Then: 'Oh!' said Rollo.

24

Sir George nodded.

'Yes, there they are.'

And he stopped the engine and they sat in silence, and looked at a sight one could see nowhere else in England: the Wild White Cattle of Clawstone Park. Madlyn had never been interested in cows. If she thought of them at all she imagined stolid, square-rumped animals who stood humbly in stalls with machines clamped to their udders and said 'Moo'.

But these creatures were not like that. They were not like that at all.

They stood in the shade of a clump of oaks and every line of their bodies – the graceful lift of their heads, the long legs of the calves standing beside their mothers, the proud strength of the wide-horned bulls – spoke of grace and nimbleness and speed.

'I was stupid,' said Madlyn to herself. 'I didn't understand.'

Where they had come from, these fabled beasts, no one knew. Some said a ship from Spain had been wrecked on the coast and the cattle had swum ashore and made their way across the hills to Clawstone. Others said they were descended from the wide-horned aurochs who had lived in the primeval forests of the north. Whatever their beginnings, the cattle had roamed free inside the seven hundred acres of Clawstone Park as long as anyone could remember – and the owners of Clawstone had protected them.

But they protected them from a distance, for the creatures were as wild as wolves. No one milked them; they were never brought inside in bad weather or to have their calves; no one fed them cattle cake or took them to the vet – indeed, it could be dangerous to handle them; they could not endure the touch of human beings.

And each and every one was as white as snow.

'Can we get out?' asked Rollo.

'No. But we can go closer.'

It was like an African safari as they drove slowly towards the herd, hoping they would not take flight.

'They were the cattle of the ancient Druids,' said Sir George, and it was easy to imagine how those wise wanderers would have prized such a herd, both as givers of food and as a source of sacrifice. It was always white bulls that the gods wanted when they thirsted for blood.

They had come very near to the herd. Sir George turned off the engine and they let down the windows as far as they would go. The king bull stared at them, unafraid, knowing that nothing could threaten him. Beside him grazed the oldest of the cows, with her scars and her crumpled horn. Two calves butted each other, playing; another drank from its mother, who flicked the flies from him with her tail. One cow was lying down a little way from the rest; a salad of dark green plants hung from her mouth.

'Are those stinging nettles she's eating?' asked Rollo.

Sir George nodded. 'Cows know what plants are good for them, especially when they're going to have their calves. She's due any day now.' They watched in silence. Then quite suddenly the herd took off, the king bull leading, stampeding across the shallow ford, racing away towards the high ground.

'Was it us?' asked Rollo, worried.

Sir George shook his head and pointed. A red deer,

an antlered stag, had appeared between the trees.

'They'll take off suddenly like that if anything startles them.'

Rollo said nothing as they drove back through the gates, and nothing when they returned to the castle. In silence he made his way up the main staircase, and the second flight of stairs, and the third. When he reached the top floor he walked from room to room till he found a window that overlooked the park and the hill where the cattle were grazing. Then he pulled a table over to the window and found a chair, which he put on top of the table, and climbed on to it and pressed his nose against the glass.

Sir George found him there an hour later. Rollo's eyes were dreamy, his nose was pale where the blood had left it.

'Are they always white?' he asked his great-uncle. 'Always and for ever?'

'Yes. Always. They have bred true for a thousand years.'

Rollo nodded. 'Are they your cows? Do they belong to you?'

'They belong to themselves. But I guard them.'

Then: 'I will help you,' said Rollo.

Five

On the Saturday when Madlyn first helped to sell tickets for Open Day, exactly twelve people came to look over Clawstone Castle. And on the same Saturday, the number of people who went to visit Trembellow Towers, just twelve kilometres away, was three hundred and four.

Not that Lord Trembellow had to count heads the way they did at Clawstone. He had set up an electric turnstile at the entrance to the house, which relayed the number of visitors directly to his office. Trembellow might be his home but he ran it as a business.

He ran everything as a business; his home, his wife and children and, of course, the firms he owned: the cone manufacturing factory, the road haulage business, the quarries and the gravel pits. There was hardly an hour in the day or night when one of his lorries was not roaring up and down the roads of Britain, or one of his shovellers was not digging into a hillside or one of his cement mixers was not helping to spew out concrete.

Lord Trembellow had been born Arthur Ackerly in Newcastle upon Tyne. His father worked on the coal barges which plied up and down the Tyne; there had been seven children to feed, and Arthur had done wonderfully well, so if he was pleased with himself – and he certainly was – no one could blame him.

When he bought Trembellow Towers, he was determined that it should be the most outstanding, the largest and the most visited castle in Britain. It was not an old building like Clawstone; it looked in fact as though the hill it stood on had come out in enormous, red brick boils. Even so, it was not large enough or showy enough for Lord Trembellow. He added two towers to the ones that were already there and dug a moat and built a drawbridge. He had battlements put on the roof and built a minstrels' gallery and enlarged the banqueting hall.

The museum at Trembellow did not exhibit stuffed ducks that had choked on sticklebacks or gas-mask cases left over from the war. It showed priceless swords and body armour and jewelled saddles. The visitors who came to Trembellow thought, of course, that these things had belonged to the family for generations, but actually Lord Trembellow's grown-up son Neville, who lived in London and was a banker, had bought them at antiques auctions. Neville had bought pictures of the ancestors that hung in the dining room too. They were nothing whatever to do with the Trembellows, but one ancestor is much like another and nobody guessed.

Visitors to Trembellow did not have to stumble round the castle on their own as they did at Clawstone. They had proper guides who made little speeches in each of the rooms. There was piped music in the tea rooms and everything sold in the gift shop was stamped with the Trembellow crest. You can buy a coat of arms from the College of Heralds when you become a lord and Lord Trembellow had done just that.

'Well, my little sugar plum,' he said now, coming into the dining room for his lunch, 'we've beaten our record. Three hundred and four visitors!'

His 'little sugar plum' was his ten-year-old daughter Olive, and it was hard to imagine anyone less sugary or less like a plum. Her skin was sallow, she was thin with a pursed mouth and small black eyes, and the inside of her brain might have been a calculator.

'We shall do even better next Saturday,' she said now.

Olive was a great comfort to her father. She was small but she did not look young; she looked like a shrunken company director, carried a briefcase even in the house and was so clever that she could almost have taken over the family business then and there.

'I've had trouble with one of the waitresses in the tea room,' said Lady Trembellow, sighing. 'She spilled tea on a woman's lap.'

'Well, sack her for goodness' sake, Phyllis. You're far too soft,' said her husband.

And Olive said, 'Yes, mother, you're far too soft. Neville says so too.'

'I suppose I am,' said Lady Trembellow sadly.

She had been very happy in the small semi in Newcastle in which she and Arthur had first lived, and happy in the detached house in the suburbs to which they moved next, but as the houses they lived in grew larger she did not feel happier. She tried very hard to keep up with her husband, who wanted her to be young and thin, and every so often, just to please him, she went off to London to see a fashionable doctor who made women more beautiful. Lady Trembellow knew that plastic surgeons had done wonderful

30

things in the war, repairing the horrific wounds that servicemen had suffered, so she trusted this doctor completely and did everything he suggested. She had a facelift and she had some fat removed from her thighs and a tuck put in her tummy – but she did not feel younger or more beautiful. She felt as though everything was very *tight*.

'I'm sure we'll be up to three hundred and fifty visitors by the end of the month,' said Olive. 'And the Clawstone visitors will be down to ten . . . and then five . . . and then nobody!'

'That's right, my little pigeon,' said her fond father. 'We'll put that ramshackle place completely out of business. And that'll be the end of the Percivals and their stupid cattle . . . They can send the cows to be slaughtered and we'll throw them out and take over.'

He rubbed his hands. When he first moved to Trembellow he had opened his house to the public because he wanted to show off his wealth and his possessions, and beating Sir George was good sport.

But since then he and his son Neville had come up with an excellent idea. The grounds of Clawstone Castle would make a perfect building site for a new housing estate. Nothing fancy – just two hundred or so houses close together and a supermarket and a garage.

Clawstone was twelve kilometres away, so one wouldn't see the new development from the windows at Trembellow; there was a hill in the way and a wood. There was no danger that he or his family would have to look at rows of houses lived in by people who wouldn't know how to make their gardens nice – if indeed there was room for gardens, which there probably wouldn't be.

He had done the sums: two hundred houses would bring in a cool ten million pounds.

But first he had to turn out Sir George – and of course the blasted cattle they made such a fuss about. And that meant ruining the Percivals and driving them away from Clawstone. That the best building land in Britain should be grazed over by cows was ridiculous. It was an outrage. Something would have to be done, Lord Trembellow told himself – and he was the man to do it.

Six

Rollo was a faithful person. He did not forget to feed his caterpillars and he went on putting out saucers of milk for the hedgehog. Hardly a day passed when he did not visit the badger's sett by the stream and he went on writing letters to his skink.

But he had told his great-uncle that he would guard the cattle – and that was what he did. He knew he must not go into the park alone, that the animals could be dangerous, but he could stand by the gate in the wall that surrounded it, and watch, and this is what he did, often for hours at a time.

And when he had to be indoors he went on watching. He had his special cow-watching places: the library steps in the book room and the old table in one of the attics, on to which he had put a kitchen chair. The book room faced east and the attic faced west so that he could follow the cattle as they wandered through their domain. It was only when they were deep in a cluster of trees that he lost sight of them.

The day after Rollo had first been to the park Sir George brought him a pair of binoculars, much smaller than the usual ones. 'My father had them made for me when I was a boy. Try them,' he said.

Rollo took the ancient leather case and lifted them out. Small as they were, he still found them hard to hold. Then suddenly he screwed the focusing knob

33

the right way – and in an instant the face of a calf leaning against his mother's side swam towards him, so close that he could have touched it.

'Oh!' said Rollo. 'I can see his wet nose . . . and his ear.'

Sir George said no more but he had to turn away from Rollo because he was so moved. He had felt himself to be very much alone, but now it seemed that there was someone else – someone of his own blood – who felt as he did about the cattle. Perhaps if he could only hold out for a few years, Rollo would take over. Perhaps there would be another member of the family who would see the cattle as a sacred trust, to be protected and kept from harm.

George and Emily had been brought up to think that it was not polite to talk about money. They would not have thought it right to let the children know how desperately hard up they were and how important it was to get what they could from the visitors, so it was Ned who answered Madlyn's questions.

'It's the cattle, you see. They cost the earth to keep up and Sir George'll – he'll never sell them or let them go. He won't even charge people to go into the park and look at them. You could make quite a bit that way; there's plenty of people ask to see them, but he'll never take a penny when he shows them round.'

'But why? Why are they so expensive?' asked Madlyn. 'They just eat grass, don't they, and the grass is there?'

'Well, it is and it isn't. Grass is a crop like anything else. They can't use any artificial spray or fertilizer on it because it might harm the beasts. Everything has to be done by hand, and that's terribly expensive. And

34

the walls of the park have to be repaired, and the warden paid.'

The warden, Bernie, was Ned's uncle – and Ned knew as much as anybody about the upkeep of the cattle.

'You don't think Rollo's *too* fond of the cows?' asked Madlyn. 'He's sort of besotted. As though . . . they're creatures from another world.'

'Rollo's all right,' said Ned. 'No need to worry about him. Come to that, there's a lot of people who feel as though the cows are special. They've been here so long, it's like having a bit of history right here. My Ma reckons if the cattle went, the village would become a sort of ghost town.'

Meanwhile the summer took its course; bees hung from the flowers, the lime trees gave off a marvellous scent, high white clouds rode across the sky. But if the countryside was beautiful, what was happening inside the castle was very worrying indeed. Because the Honourable Olive had been right: more and more visitors came to Trembellow and fewer and fewer came to Clawstone.

But it wasn't till she went upstairs to help Aunt Emily sort out the things for the gift shop that Madlyn saw that something would have to be done.

Emily was sitting on the bed. Beside her on the quilt were the three lavender bags, the tea cosy made of Uncle George's pyjamas, a glove with four fingers, and a bookmark stuck with pressed periwinkle flowers.

And Emily was crying.

When she saw Madlyn she hurriedly dabbed her eyes but it wasn't easy to fool Madlyn, who came and put her arm round Emily's shoulders and said, 'What is it, Aunt Emily? What's the matter?'

Emily waved an arm at the treasures on the counterpane.

'Nothing has sold, Madlyn. Nothing. Not one thing. And I'm so tired, and I can't think of anything else to make. It's all hopeless, and it will break George's heart if we have to sell the park. He seems to think the cows came to him from God.' She groped for a handkerchief and blew her nose. 'Before they opened up Trembellow we could just keep going, but now . . .'

Madlyn moved the lavender bags and sat down beside her aunt. Part of her was feeling rather cross. She had so many friends at school that she worried about and cared about, and there were her parents and Rollo. Loving people is hard work and she had not intended to start caring about her ancient aunt. But she did care about her – and now it seemed that something would have to be done.

Only what? What would bring visitors flocking to Clawstone? Not more lavender bags, that was for sure, not more burnt scones or tea cosies . . . What would turn people away from Trembellow and bring them to Clawstone?

When she went to bed that night Madlyn tossed and turned for hours, racking her brains . . . Then suddenly she sat up in bed. Of course. She should have thought of it before. It was obvious.

When she had an idea now, Madlyn discussed it with Ned.

'Well, I suppose you're right. But I don't know where we'd get them from. There aren't any in the village as far as I know.'

'Why not? You'd think there'd be plenty. People must have drowned in the horse pond or been murdered in dark lanes or buried in the wrong graves.'

Ned was pondering. 'I dare say, but I suppose this is a quiet sort of place and they just stayed in the ground or wherever.'

'I'll have to ask Cousin Howard,' said Madlyn. 'He must know.'

Ned looked at her sideways. 'I'd better come with you. He can be a bit moody like.'

'All right. I'd be glad if you would, actually. I've never talked to him properly and Aunt Emily doesn't realize that I know what he is.'

Cousin Howard was in his library and not pleased to be disturbed. They had brought Rollo also, and when he saw the three children he hurried away quickly and vanished through the door that led into his bedroom.

But this time the children took no notice. 'Please, Cousin Howard, we need your help,' said Madlyn. 'We really need it.'

Cousin Howard reappeared through the door. He was wearing his usual dressing gown and leather slippers, and his face, which was always pale, had turned quite white with panic and alarm.

'I'm not . . . I don't talk to people I don't know . . .' he mumbled. 'I don't talk to people that I *do* know. I don't talk.'

He took out a handkerchief and mopped his brow. He had the long scholarly features of the Percivals, and his straggly grey hair was badly in need of cutting.

Howard had lived most of his life at Clawstone, but like all the Percival men he had been sent away to boarding school when he was a boy, where he had been most unhappy . . .

'What's the *point* of Percival, can anyone tell me?' one of the prefects had sneered when he first saw Howard. 'I mean, what's he *for*?'

No one knew the answer to that, and all through his time at school Howard had been called Pointless Percival. That kind of thing can leave its mark and it was not surprising that Howard was so withdrawn and shy and spent his life sorting and cataloguing books. But though the children were sorry for him, they had no time to waste.

'Cousin Howard, we've got to do something to make more people come to the castle. We've simply got to,' said Madlyn. 'Otherwise the cattle will have to be sold and maybe the castle too and—'

'Oh, don't say that!' The thought of leaving his home made poor Howard tremble.

'So we have to find a way of attracting more visitors, and we thought if we could show them some proper ghosts – real spectres – they'd come and tell their friends and—'

A heart-rending wail – a wail of true despair – came from Cousin Howard.

'Oh, no . . . No! It's impossible. It is quite out of the question. George has asked me, and Emily too – but I've had to refuse. Showing myself to all those people . . . Appearing and disappearing. I couldn't. I absolutely couldn't.'

And he began to shiver so badly that his outline became quite blurred.

The children looked at each other. They were very distressed by the misunderstanding, and the pain they had caused poor Howard.

'We don't mean you, Cousin Howard,' said Madlyn.

'We wouldn't think of asking you,' said Rollo reassuringly.

'We need *proper* ghosts. Really scary ones with . . . oh, you know, heads that come off, and daggers in their chests, and that kind of thing,' said Ned – and then blushed because it seemed rude to suggest that Howard was not a proper ghost.

But Cousin Howard was terribly relieved. 'Oh, I see. Well, that's all right then. I really don't think I would do, you know. I tripped on my dressing-gown cord on the stairs and broke my neck, but it was a clean break – there's no blood or anything.' He bent his head and leaned forward to show them, and really there was hardly anything to see – just a slight dent in the ectoplasm. 'And I have never felt inclined to gibber or howl or anything like that,' Howard went on. 'It isn't what I *do*. But if it isn't me you want, why have you come?'

'We thought you might know where we could find some other ghosts. The kind that would be terrifying,' said Madlyn. 'We thought you might have friends.'

Howard was shocked. 'Friends! Oh, dear me no! I don't have friends. I don't go out much, you see. I hardly ever go out.'

But the children just looked at him steadily.

'Please could you try and help us?' said Madlyn. 'Please?'

'It's for the cows,' said Rollo.

Seven

Olive Trembellow was perfectly correct, as she always was. On the following Open Day there were three hundred and fifty visitors to Trembellow – and the number of visitors going to Clawstone was down to seven.

So now she was doing what she liked best in all the world.

She was doing sums.

She was multiplying the number of visitors who had come to Trembellow on the last Open Day by the amount each of them had paid, and the answer was coming to a figure with a lot of noughts at the end. Olive liked figures with noughts on the end. She liked them very much.

When she had checked her calculations she went to see her father in his study.

Lord Trembellow was doing business with his son Neville, who had come up from London, and a builder he had brought with him, but he didn't mind being interrupted. Olive was almost a business partner herself.

'Look, Daddy – we've taken nearly four thousand pounds today. We had three hundred and fifty visitors and Clawstone only had seven – and one of those was a spy.'

Lord Trembellow nodded. He had sent one of his

staff, a man who was new to the district and would not be recognized, to join the visitors going round Clawstone.

'You've never seen such a ramshackle place,' he had told Lord Trembellow when he came back. 'They've just got a kid taking the tickets, and no guides or anything. And the rubbish in the museum – you wouldn't believe it. There's a sewing machine and a jar of caterpillars and something called a Hoggart.'

'What's a Hoggart?' Lord Trembellow had asked.

'I don't know, my lord. It's a thing like half a skinned Pekinese rolled into a sort of ball and it's just labelled "The Clawstone Hoggart".'

Lord Trembellow turned to his son. 'Get me one of those in London, will you? If they've got a Hoggart I'll have one too. No, get me two Hoggarts.'

'Why only two, Daddy?' asked Olive. 'Why not three . . . or five . . . ?'

'Good idea, my little sugar plum. Make a note of it, Neville. Five Hoggarts.'

Spread out on the desk in the study was an aerial photograph of the district. It had been taken from a helicopter and showed the grounds of Clawstone very clearly: the castle, the gardens – and the park surrounded by its high wall. If one looked carefully one could just make out the specks of the cattle.

Neville and the builder were bending over it while Lord Trembellow told them his plans.

'As soon as I've got old Percival out I'll get it properly surveyed, but this shows enough. The park's a perfect building site; the drainage is good and so's the soil – no danger of flooding. There's room for two hundred houses easily.'

'Why just two hundred houses, Daddy?' said Olive in her high, prim voice. 'Why not three hundred? Or even four? People like that wouldn't mind living close together. Then we'd get twice as much money.'

'Well, maybe.' He smiled fondly at his daughter. Some people's children were a disappointment to them, but Olive was exactly the kind of daughter he had wished for.

'We'd have to get round the planning people but I dare say it could be done. And then – in with the bulldozers, cut down the trees, lay concrete everywhere . . . make things tidy.'

Lord Trembellow loved concrete. Grass and flowers and trees were so messy. Grass needed cutting, flowers could give you hay fever and trees blew down in the wind. But concrete . . . concrete was smooth and trouble-free, concrete gave you a level surface.

When he thought of the countryside covered in giant cement mixers pouring out streams of the wonderful stuff, Lord Trembellow was a happy man.

Lady Trembellow was quite different. She longed for a garden and she loved animals – again and again she asked her husband if they couldn't get a dog. But his answer was always 'No', and when she tried to argue he changed the subject.

'It's time you went to London again and had something done about your nose,' he would say. Or he would suggest that she had the cartilage in her ears cut so as to make them lie flatter against her head.

And because she had been brought up to think that a wife must please her husband, Lady Trembellow said no more.

Eight

The children had come away from Cousin Howard feeling very discouraged.

'I suppose we were silly to think he could do anything,' said Madlyn. 'He's led such a sheltered life.'

They didn't try to see him again and he didn't come out of his room. But three days after they had waylaid him in his library, something strange happened. The children didn't see it – they were in bed and asleep – but Sir George saw it and it surprised him very much.

Just as the clock struck midnight an old rusty bicycle with upright handlebars rode slowly out of the lumber room and crossed the courtyard. There was nobody on it, and nobody pushing it, but the pedals could be seen to move and the un-oiled wheels gave off an occasional tired squeak.

Quite by itself, with only the slightest of wobbles, the riderless bicycle made its way towards the gateway, turned into the drive and was gone.

'Well, well,' said Sir George, moving away from the window. 'Who would have thought it? It must be years since Howard went out at night.'

Some ten kilometres south of Clawstone stood an old rambling house completely covered in ivy. The house was called Greenwood and it belonged to an old lady

43

called Mrs Lee-Perry, who lived there alone.

Mrs Lee-Perry was immensely ancient; she was quite transparent with age; her voice was hoarse and faint, her wrists were as thin as matchsticks and it took her nearly five minutes to get up from her chair.

But she was not dead. She should have been – she was only a year off her hundredth birthday – but she was not.

The trouble was that all her friends *were*. Her husband was dead and her brother was dead and all the many friends who used come to her house. Mrs Lee-Perry loved music and poetry and she had been famous for her Thursday Evening Gatherings when people played together and sang together and read aloud from books that they enjoyed.

So when the last of the friends who had come to her Thursday Gatherings had passed away, Mrs Lee-Perry almost perished from sheer loneliness.

But one day as she hobbled into her drawing room she found something unexpected. She found an old friend of hers, Colonel Hickley, sitting at the piano playing one of the tunes they had liked to sing at her Gatherings. And this was very interesting because Colonel Hickley was dead. He had passed away two years earlier and she had been to his funeral.

Which meant that he was a ghost.

And that was the beginning. Because if Colonel Hickley could still make music though he was a ghost, so could all her other friends: Admiral Hardmann, who had died on the hunting field, and Signora Fresca, who had been a soprano in Italy before she came to live in the north of England, and Fifi Fenwick, who bred bull terriers and had played the violin quite beautifully . . .

It had taken a while to find everybody and this was because the friends she was looking for were *quiet* ghosts, the kind that had finished with their lives and just drifted about peacefully. (It is the *unquiet* ghosts one hears about: the ones who have died angrily and have unfinished business in the world.) But Colonel Hickley had been most helpful and now her Thursday Gatherings were in full swing once again. Of course, she had not said anything to her neighbours or to the cleaning lady. She just saw to it that the curtains were drawn and let it be known that she was not to be disturbed, and if the people in the village guessed something, they kept quiet, for Mrs Lee-Perry was very much respected and what she did on Thursday evening was entirely her own affair.

It goes without saying that Cousin Howard had been invited – he was known to recite poetry very beautifully and he played both the piano and the organ – but he had only come once or twice because of his dreadful shyness and the feeling that no one could really want a person who had been known for years as Pointless Percival.

But now he rode his ancient bicycle up the drive of Greenwood, rang the bell and glided up to the drawing room.

He had come during a break in the music and everyone was pleased to see him.

'Well, well, my friend, this is a pleasure,' said Mrs Lee-Perry. 'I hope everybody is well at Clawstone? Dear George and dear Emily?'

45

'And the dear cows?' asked Fifi Fenwick, who was a great animal lover.

'Yes . . . er . . . yes . . . Except that . . .'

But he was too shy to explain at once that Clawstone was in trouble and that he had come to ask for help, so he took the sheet of music which Admiral Hardmann handed him and joined in the bass part of a song called 'A Maying We Will Go' and another one called 'Let the Sackbuts Sound and Thunder'. After that Signora Fresca warbled through an aria about a betrayed bullfighter and then they begged Howard to recite 'On Hill and Dale a Maiden Wandered', which was very moving and sad.

Everybody clapped when he had finished – a strange rustling noise made with their ghostly hands – and said that no one could speak poetry like he did, and it was now that Howard, stammering a little, explained how difficult things were at Clawstone and that the children who had come to stay at the castle had had an idea which they thought might make more people come to Open Day.

But when he had finished the ancient figures filling the room looked at him with amazement.

'My dear Howard,' said Admiral Hardmann, 'I hope you don't think that *we* would come and haunt Clawstone?'

'We would hardly be suitable for that kind of thing,' said Miss Netherfield, who had been a headmistress. 'It sounds like *romping about* and we are definitely not . . . rompers.'

'No, no!' said Cousin Howard, and his ectoplasm became quite pink with embarrassment. And indeed the room full of elderly and respectable ghosts, with their hearing aids and walking sticks, would not have done much to bring people in on Open Day. 'Oh, dear me no, not at all. But they wanted me to find . . . those rather vulgar ghosts . . . the kind that, er . . . scream and . . . take off their heads and so on. And I don't get about much. I wondered if any of you . . . the Admiral might know more people . . . or have servants who know . . .'

Poor Howard stammered and was silent. But Mrs Lee-Perry smiled at him kindly. She had known the Percivals all her life.

'Come, come,' she said to her ghostly friends. 'Surely you can think of a few suitable ones.'

Fifi Fenwick sighed. 'I do remember some story about a stabbed bride . . . Or perhaps she was shot. Cynthia's girl. It was a while ago but she's probably around somewhere.'

'And there was some young man over near Carlisle, ended in a dungeon,' said Colonel Hickley. 'Can't quite remember it now but it was a nasty story.'

'Well, see what you can do,' said Mrs Lee-Perry. And her guests thanked her for a lovely evening and glided out into the night.

Nine

'She's had her calf!' said Rollo, rushing upstairs to find Madlyn. 'The cow who eats stinging nettles . . . It tried to stand up at once and then it fell down and stood up again and started to drink but the mother kept licking it so hard that it fell over again. I saw it all from the top of the wall.' Rollo had found a flat place on the top of the wall round the park which he could reach from the overhanging branch of an elm tree. 'The herd's the biggest now it's been for ten years.'

Yes, but for how long? thought Madlyn. *How long will there be a herd?* And for the first time since she had come, she was wishing it was time to go back home to London. Because nothing as far as she could see could now save Clawstone. At the last Open Day there had been five visitors and one of them was an old man who lived in the village and was sorry for the Percivals.

And Cousin Howard had been useless. The few times they had seen him since they'd asked for his help he had hurried away without speaking. But the next morning, just as the children were making their way downstairs, they met him again and this time he didn't glide away; he actually stopped and beckoned to them.

'There are a few . . . people . . . you might like to see,' he said in his quiet, shy voice. 'This afternoon, perhaps?'

So they went to tell Ned and as soon as lunch was over they made their way to Cousin Howard's library.

As they sat down, facing the big wall of books at one end of the room, they didn't really know what they were expecting, but in fact they had been invited to hold an audition.

'I don't want you to choose anyone . . . er . . . unsuitable,' said Cousin Howard. 'If . . . somebody . . . doesn't fit your requirements they can be sent back. But the . . . ones that will appear are willing to come and . . . do what you ask.' He cleared his throat. 'I shall call them one by one if that is convenient.'

The children nodded and Madlyn moved her chair a little closer to Rollo's. She didn't think he would be nervous; he was not a nervous boy, but she wanted to be near him just in case.

Cousin Howard clapped his hands. There was a pause. Then slowly . . . very slowly . . . there appeared a long, white floating veil . . . a wreath of wilted orange blossom . . . and then: a face.

The bride who stood before them was very beautiful, but she was quite shockingly bloodied. There was blood on her veil, blood on her dress, blood on her train and her silver shoes.

And there was a good reason for this. There was a bullet hole in her left cheek, another in her chest, a third in her arm.

Cousin Howard introduced her. 'This is Brenda Peabody. She had some . . . er . . . trouble on her wedding day. A man she had jilted shot her on the steps of the church.'

'Trouble?' spat the ghost. 'Oh yes, I had some trouble! Men . . . Vile beasts! Look at that!' She dug

49

her fingers into the holes, and fresh streams of blood poured over her bridal clothes. 'And it won't come *out* . . . I wash and I scrub and it makes no difference, the gore just goes on coming. Drip, drip . . . ooze, ooze.'

'I don't know if you have heard of banshees?' said Cousin Howard quietly. 'They're famous for weeping and wailing and washing out the linen of the dead. Brenda's not a banshee, of course, she's a proper ghost and she's busy with her own washing, but one thing you can be sure of with Bloodstained Brides is a constant stream of liquid. She won't dry up, you can be certain of that.'

'She's good,' said Madlyn. 'She's very good.' Brenda disappeared behind the books and when Cousin Howard clapped his hands again a dark shape in an enormous duffel coat appeared.

'This is Mr Smith.'

The children looked at each other. So far Mr Smith didn't seem very remarkable – just a very fat man in a heavy coat.

Then Mr Smith said, 'Pleased to meet you,' and at the same time he threw his overcoat wide open and lowered his hood.

He was a skeleton. A few pieces of flesh still clung to him here and there, a small slab of muscle below one knee, and a sinew or two on his elbow . . . and in one eye socket there still hung a single eye – but overall Mr Smith was as skeletal a skeleton as you could find.

All three children nodded their heads. If there is one thing people expect from a haunted house it is a skeleton, and a skeleton in which one eye still flickers is particularly good.

Mr Smith, whose first name was Douglas, had been a very fat taxi driver – so fat that people had nagged him and teased him, and he was so hurt that he stopped eating. Only he overdid it, and one day he woke up dead. When you have been very fat it is difficult to accept that you are now very thin or even not there at all, which was why Doug liked to wear his overcoat.

After the bride and the skeleton came a very old woman from whose matted, grimy hair there dropped a stream of lice.

Real lice are nasty and ghostly lice are nastier still, but all the same the old woman did not look very interesting. Nasty, yes, but not interestingly nasty, and the children were very relieved when she said she'd decided that Clawstone wouldn't suit her and she was going back to live with her cronies in the bus shelter behind the slaughterhouse in town.

The next candidate surprised the children very much.

She was a truly beautiful girl, with masses of jet-black hair and lustrous dark eyes ringed with kohl and she was wearing a short embroidered bodice, loose trousers of shimmering silk and brocade slippers.

'This is Sunita,' said Cousin Howard. 'Her parents came from India but she has lived here all her life. And worked here too.'

The three children stared at her and Sunita smiled, a lovely friendly smile, and put her hands together in greeting. Everybody liked her at once; you couldn't not like her. But Rollo spoke for all of them when he said, 'Would she frighten people? She seems so nice.'

'Watch,' said Cousin Howard.

He nodded at the girl, and she took a step forward, so that they could see the jewel in her tummy button and her golden-brown midriff. Then, as they stared, a sudden jagged line appeared round her middle – an irregular streak, like lightning, which turned darker and more sinister as they watched. And slowly . . . very slowly . . . the top half of Sunita floated upwards to the ceiling, leaving the bottom half still firmly on the ground.

'She was sawn in half,' whispered Cousin Howard. 'The man she worked for did it. It was a trick in a circus – you know . . . sawing a girl in half. It's often done, but this time it went wrong and he really halved her. Poor man, he was dreadfully upset, but it was too late.'

Everyone, of course, wanted Sunita; she passed the audition straight away. After her came a very boring ghost, a hoity-toity lady in a hooped petticoat who didn't seem able to do much and whom they had to send away. But after that came Ranulf de Torqueville.

Ranulf was dressed in old-fashioned clothes: velvet breeches and a loose white shirt. His hair was long and he looked romantic, like the people one sees in swashbuckling films having sword fights and leaping from high walls.

'What does he do?' asked Rollo.

They were soon to know. With an agonized grimace, Ranulf opened his shirt. And there, hanging on to his chest, its front legs scrabbling at the bare skin, its scabrous tail thrashing, was a huge black rat, gnawing at his heart.

'He was cursed,' explained Cousin Howard. 'His

evil brother said, "May rats gnaw at your heart till you die," and threw him in a dungeon. Only in this particular case the rat died too. It is not usual for a rat to hang on like that, but you can't separate them; it never lets go.'

'It's a proper plague rat,' said Rollo. '*Rattus rattus*. The kind that first came over in ships and caused the Black Death. The brown rats came later.'

But even Rollo, fond of animals as he was, could hardly bear to look at the twitching, yellow-toothed creature tearing and scrunching and clawing at the young man's heart.

'I think we've got enough now,' said Ned when they had agreed that Ranulf would do splendidly. 'Four ghosts seems about right,' and the others agreed. But just as they were getting up to go, a pair of feet suddenly appeared from behind the wall. They were large feet: hairy, bare and not very clean. And nothing at all was attached to them. No ankles, no knees, no thighs, and certainly no body. They were simply feet.

'Oh dear, I told them they wouldn't do. I told *both* feet.' Cousin Howard was looking worried. 'I didn't see what could be done simply with feet.'

But the feet were obstinate. They were determined. Every time they were told to go away they returned.

'I suppose we could make room for them,' said Madlyn. 'I mean, just feet don't take up a lot of space.'

'Maybe they feel they've been *chosen*,' said Rollo. 'It's a thing that happens.'

So the final list contained the Bride called Brenda, Mr Smith the Skeleton, Sawn-in-half Sunita, Ranulf with his rat – and The Feet.

There was nothing left now except to thank Cousin

Howard for finding the ghosts, and this they did again and again.

'You must have taken so much trouble,' said Madlyn.

And Cousin Howard said, no, no, not really, he had been only too glad to help.

Aunt Emily and Uncle George had of course noticed the change in Cousin Howard. No one now would have called him Pointless Percival – or Pointless anything at all. He spent more and more time out of his room; he glided round the castle looking busy and purposeful. The Hoggart was forgotten.

'When did you realize that Cousin Howard was . . . not quite like us?' Aunt Emily asked the children.

'Oh, quite soon,' said Madlyn. 'After a few days – only we didn't like to say anything.'

But now seemed to be a good time to mention their plans for the next Open Day and to ask their great-aunt and great-uncle whether they minded if a few of Cousin Howard's acquaintances came to help bring in more visitors.

'What do you think, dear?' Aunt Emily asked her brother.

Sir George was worrying about some loose stones he had found in the wall of the park and not really listening very hard.

'I suppose it can't do any harm. As long as they're proper ghosts. No cheating.'

'Oh, they're proper ghosts all right, Uncle George,' said Rollo. 'You can't get more proper ghosts than these!'

Ten

With only three days to go till Open Day the children started rehearsals for the haunting straight away – and it was very hard work.

Brenda made it clear that she didn't just want to drip blood on to people – she wanted to strangle them and put her icy hands round their throats and tighten them till they choked.

'Round *men's* throats,' she said firmly.

Mr Smith was still in a muddle about his size.

'I can't fit in there,' he said, when Madlyn suggested that he might like to lie in the oak chest in the Great Hall because it was the nearest thing they had to a coffin.

'But, Mr Smith, you're a *skeleton*,' said Madlyn. 'You can't *be* thinner than that.'

'Oh yes, I forgot.'

When you have been as fat as Mr Smith had been, it is difficult to realize how much you have changed.

Most skeletons are not interesting to talk to because they can't use proper words; they just rattle their bones and grind their teeth. But Mr Smith, like all the ghosts that Cousin Howard had found, was special, and had kept the deep and matey voice he had had when he was a taxi driver.

Ranulf spent a lot of time buttoning and unbuttoning his shirt.

'I could open it suddenly, with a flourish,' he said, 'so that the rat, so to speak, exploded in people's faces.'

But when they said yes, that would be good, he thought that maybe unbuttoning it slowly might be better. 'So that that the tail appeared first,' he said, 'and then the legs . . .'

Because she had worked in a circus, Sunita had a real feeling for special effects. What the children loved particularly was the little sigh she gave just before she separated herself into two halves; it made the whole thing very moving and beautiful.

Which left The Feet. No one knew quite what to do with them and they were standing about rather wearily when the kitchen door opened and a blast of sound from Mrs Grove's radio came out towards them.

It was a Scottish reel. A special one. The reel of the 51st Highlanders played on the bagpipes.

For a moment nothing happened. Then the left toes began to tap, followed by the toes on the right . . . and The Feet began to dance. The toes rose and fell, they curled and uncurled. The heels thumped on the floor, the ankle stumps crossed and uncrossed . . . and all in perfect time to the music.

All Highland reels need to be practised if one is to do them well, but the reel of the 51st Highlanders is the most difficult of all. And here were these ancient hairy feet, with their corns and their calluses, dancing as if to the manner born.

Clearly these were Scottish feet – feet from over the border. Having feet like these at Clawstone could only be an honour, and they decided to bring up Ned's CD player and let The Feet do what they felt like on the day.

Rehearsing a show too much can be as bad as rehearsing one too little.

The ghosts which Cousin Howard had found had one thing in common: all of them were homeless.

Ranulf's dungeon had been blown up and a shoe factory built on the site. Brenda, who had liked to haunt the graveyard behind the church where she'd been shot, left it when a motorway was driven through it. Mr Smith's flat near the taxi rank was bought by a couple who started doing what they called 'improvements', which meant knocking down perfectly good walls, putting up partitions and painting the woodwork in colours which made his skull ache. And Sunita's family had washed their hands of her when she went to work in a circus.

So the first thing the children did was to try and make the ghosts feel comfortable in the castle and give them a place they could call their own.

They offered them the dungeon and the armoury and the banqueting hall – but the ghosts chose the old nursery at the very top of the house. There was a day nursery with a Wendy house and a dappled rocking horse and a tinny piano, and a night nursery with three small beds and a sagging sofa and a row of china chamber pots. There was also a pantry and a scullery where the children's nannies had prepared their food and washed their nappies.

'Are you sure this is what you want?' Madlyn asked, because the rooms, though dusty and full of cobwebs, were light and cheerful. 'You wouldn't rather have somewhere damp and dark?'

But the ghosts liked the white-painted rooms,

which had belonged to the Percival children long ago. It reminded them of the times before they had grown up, and suffered, and become phantoms. Ranulf spent much of the time on the dappled horse – he said that the rocking movement quietened the rat – and Brenda was pleased with the big sink where she could soak her veil and dab at the spots on her dress. She had told them that she had been a war bride and married at a time when clothes were rationed and one had to save up for them not only with money but with coupons.

'Thirty-three coupons, this dress cost me,' she said – and of course that made it understandable that she should be so cross about the blood.

As the big day approached everything seemed to be going really well. The ghosts kept thinking of new and interesting ways of frightening people. Ned had printed leaflets warning people to beware as some terrifying spectres had been found in Clawstone and anyone with heart problems should take care. There was even a small piece in the paper.

And then on the last evening disaster struck.

The children had gone up to the nursery to wish everybody luck – and found that the rooms were empty.

'Are you there?' they called.

But already they were alarmed. Ghosts do not usually become invisible when they are staying with friends.

At first nothing happened. Then, very slowly, the ghosts appeared. They were huddled together on the sagging sofa and they looked terrible.

'What is it? What's the matter?' asked Madlyn.

Brenda cleared her throat. 'We don't think we can

do it,' she said 'It's too difficult. It's not what we've been used to.'

'We'll never get it right,' said Mr Smith.

'Do what? What can't you do?'

'Haunt like you want us to,' said Ranulf. 'Give a proper performance. Scare people.'

The children looked at each other in dismay. They knew what they were dealing with and that it was serious.

Stage fright. The terror that can come out of the blue and attack actors and musicians before a show. Sometimes it passes, but it can be so bad that nothing on earth can make the person go on and perform. The careers of brilliant artists have been completely blighted by stage fright – and no doctor has yet found a cure.

'We don't feel we can stay,' said Ranulf, 'not if we cannot do what you ask of us.'

'It wouldn't be fair to stay if we can't do our work,' said Sunita.

Strangely, it was Rollo, who was usually so dreamy, who now took charge.

'If you come with me I'll show you why you have to help us,' he said, 'why you have to stay.'

The phantoms looked at him listlessly. The Feet stayed where they were, half buried in the sofa cushions, but the others followed him out of the nursery, down three flights of stairs and out of the castle.

He led them across the gardens, past the gate to the park and to the place where the elm tree leaned over the high stone wall. Rollo climbed up to his watching place; Madlyn and Ned followed – and the ghosts

59

glided up and settled down beside them.

They were staring down on the soft green fields of the park; the hazel and birch trees of the copse; the silver ribbon of the stream. A thrush was singing. Wild roses glowed in the hedgerows.

'There,' said Rollo. 'That's the king in front.'

The ruler of the herd came slowly out of the trees: huge and vigorous and as white as milk. Close behind him came the oldest of the cows, with her scars and her crumpled horn, followed by the others with their skittering calves. The young bull, skinny and bad-tempered, who had challenged the king so often and so unsuccessfully, came last.

'They've been safe here for a thousand years,' said Rollo, 'but if we can't get more visitors to come to the castle they'll have to be sent away – or even slaughtered. That's why you have to stay and help us.'

Sitting beside her brother, her legs dangling over the ivy-clad wall, Madlyn held her breath. Could the phantoms be expected to see what Rollo saw: beasts so special that they had to be cared for whatever the cost?

No one spoke. The park was silent; even the thrush no longer sang.

It wasn't going to work, thought Madlyn. Whatever Rollo hoped for wasn't going to happen.

But now one of the ghosts had stirred. Sunita. She rose to her feet and tossed her hair back and for a moment she stood balanced on the wall. And then she floated down, down into the field. Not the top half of her and not the bottom. All of her.

No one knows whether animals can *see* ghosts but they can certainly *sense* them. The king bull pawed

60

the ground once with his powerful hooves. The cows lifted their heads and stared. The smallest of the calves gave a sudden cry.

Sunita stood still and the cattle came forward to form a circle round her. Not crowding her, just gazing with their dark and gentle eyes. The calves stopped butting and playing and came to rest by their mothers' side. The king's great hooves were still. Every one of the beasts had its head turned to the place where she stood. Even the young and angry bull was still.

When she saw that all the animals were calm, Sunita walked up to the oldest cow, with her scars and her crumpled horn. She put her hands together and bowed down so that her hair touched the grass.

'I salute you in the name of Surabhi, the Heavenly Cow who gave birth to the sky and was the mother and muse of all created things,' she said.

Then she moved on to stand before the king bull, and on the wall the children held their breath for they knew how fierce he could be, and Sunita, down in the field, did not look like a ghost: she looked like a vulnerable girl.

'And I salute you in the name of Nandi, the bull-mount who carried the Lord God Shiva safely through the universe.'

She bowed low again and it seemed as though the bull returned her salute, bending his head so that the muscles bunched and tightened on his neck.

But Sunita had not finished. She went round the herd and to each and every beast, even the smallest of the calves, she made the same bow and spoke a greeting.

Up on the wall, the children had remembered.

'Of course,' said Ned. 'Cows are sacred in India. They wander all over the streets, and no one's allowed to harm them.'

'And when they're old they don't get slaughtered, they get sent to a place where they can live in peace. Sort of like an old people's home for cows,' said Madlyn. 'Rani told me, at school.'

Sunita, when she had returned to her place on the wall, told them more about what these beasts meant to her people.

'I was born in January,' she said. 'There's a feast then called Pongal to celebrate the harvest and the end of the rains. It goes on for days and on the third day is the Festival of Cattle. The bulls get silver caps on their horns and the cows get bead necklaces and bells and sheaves of corn. And garlands of flowers – wonderful flowers: marigolds and pinks and hibiscus blossom.'

For a moment, as they looked down on the park, the children imagined the cattle of Clawstone decorated and garlanded, with jewellery on their horns. What would Sir George say if that was to happen? Something rude, that was certain!

But Sunita had shown the ghosts something bigger than themselves. A world where animals mattered, where living things were worshipped. A world where there was work to be done and one's own troubles set aside.

'We have been selfish,' said Ranulf. 'We have not been brave. We will help you and we will stay.'

And the other ghosts nodded, and said, 'Yes, we will stay.'

Eleven

The first Open-Day-with-Ghosts began quietly – but it did not go on quietly. It did not go on quietly at all.

It had been decided that visitors should be shown round in a group rather than wander about all over the place, and Mrs Grove was appointed as the guide. She had worked in the castle so long that she knew it like the back of her hand.

As for the children, they were going to keep out of the way but watch from a hiding place in the upstairs gallery in case anything went wrong.

Because of the posters and the notice in the paper, rather more people than usual were waiting to buy tickets. There was a couple with three little girls: Lettice and Lucy and Lavinia, who chewed toffee bars and giggled as though the idea of ghosts was the funniest thing they had ever heard of.

There were two hikers: a tall thin one called Joe and a small fat one called Pete. They were on their way to a climbing trip in Scotland and had seen the notice about the ghosts and called in.

There was a sulky youth called Ham, who was on holiday with his parents and hated the country, where there was nothing to do except sit on windy beaches or walk up dripping hills, and a lady professor of architecture with her assistant, a pale girl called Angela. The professor had not come to see ghosts but to look at groynes and buttresses and mouldings.

Then there was someone who worried the children badly as they looked down from their hiding place: a delicate elderly lady called Mrs Field, who walked with two sticks and was in the charge of a muscular and bossy nurse.

'Suppose she has a heart attack?' whispered Madlyn.

'Well, we did warn people,' said Ned. 'It wouldn't be our fault.'

But the most important person in that first batch of visitors was Major Henry Hardbottock, who was a famous explorer and gave lectures and talked on the telly. Major Hardbottock had walked to the North Pole and lost two fingers from frostbite and bitten off a third when it went gangrenous; and he had walked across the Sahara without a single camel and with a raging fever. He was on his way to Edinburgh to give a lecture on 'Survival and Hardship' when he saw the notice and turned in at Clawstone just for a joke.

There was not a single person in that first group of visitors who believed in ghosts.

Mrs Grove led the party across the Inner Courtyard and into the building.

'We are now in the oldest part of the castle,' she began. 'It dates from 1423 and . . .'

She went off into her patter while Ham yawned, the little girls chewed their toffee bars and Henry Hardbottock sat on his shooting stick and looked superior.

Then: 'Eeh, look!' said Lavinia, and her mouth fell

64

open, letting out a stream of treacly goo which ran down her chin. 'Look there at that chest!'

The lid of an old oak chest had opened slowly . . . very slowly. A hand came out. An unusual hand . . .

It was the hand of a skeleton – but it was not completely bony. Small pieces of muscle still clung to it. A blob here, a strip of tissue there . . .

Not only Lavinia but Lucy and Lettice began to shriek.

'It's a skeleton!'

'It's a trick,' said Ham, sneering.

'This isn't good for you,' said the bossy nurse to little Mrs Field. 'I'll take you home.'

'No, no, it's interesting,' said the old lady, clutching her sticks. 'I don't want to go home.'

'What you are seeing is the famous Clawstone Skeleton,' said Mrs Grove. 'It is one of the oldest skeletons in England and may appear anywhere in the castle.'

Hearing himself talked about like that made Mr Smith feel brave. He was not some clapped out, overweight taxi driver; he was the Clawstone Skeleton. He pushed the lid up altogether. He sat up. He rolled his single eye. He leered.

The shrieks of the little girls grew louder.

'It's done by wires,' said Ham.

But now there stole into the noses of the visitors . . . a smell. It was a familiar smell and yet it was unexpected in this place. It was the smell of something unwashed and sweaty. At the same time the sound of music burst through the hall, and then there appeared in the doorway . . . a pair of feet.

The Feet waited for a moment as performers do

65

before they go on stage. Then they took two steps forward and began to dance; and as they danced, the smell of sweat grew stronger as the muscles strained, and the tendons pulled, and the uncut nails clacked on the flagstones – but with the most amazing rhythm, with a feeling for the music that was quite extraordinary.

'They're puppets,' sneered Ham.

The Feet danced on. As they came up to the group of people watching spellbound, they neither slowed down nor stopped. It was as though the music had bewitched them.

The lady professor gave a gulp. 'I have been *danced through* by feet,' she said in a surprised voice.

In the cloakroom, Ned changed the tape and now it was the famous reel of the 51st Highlanders which sounded out. And The Feet danced this incredibly difficult reel *up the stairs* without a single mistake – and vanished through the brocade hangings on the landing.

'We will now make our way to the dungeons,' said Mrs Grove.

The party of visitors followed her. Major Henry Hardbottock walked ahead, making it clear that he was different and important.

'It was here that prisoners were thrown,' said Mrs Grove. 'Often they fell on the bodies of men who were already dead.'

Upstairs the children, leaning over the wooden rails, looked anxiously at Mrs Field tottering gallantly after the others with her two sticks.

'I'm going to take you home,' said the bossy nurse. 'This is no place for you.'

'No, please. I want to see what comes next,' said the old lady.

What came next, as they left the dungeon, was a great cloud of steam, followed by a high-pitched and eerie wailing. Then through the steam they saw the figure of a laundry maid bending over a cauldron of water. She seemed to be wearing a white cap and a white trailing apron and through the writhing vapour they heard her curses and her moans.

'It won't come OUT,' she screamed. 'I can't get it out.'

She bent over the tub and lifted out a white cloth covered in red splashes. As soon as she scrubbed out one stain, another one appeared.

'It's blood,' whispered Lucy, clutching her sisters. 'You can see it, all gooey and red.'

But now the washing girl straightened herself and they saw that she was not wearing a cap but a bridal wreath. And her glittering eyes searched the party of visitors.

'Men!' she spat. 'It's men I want. Men have betrayed me and now I shall get my revenge.'

Dripping water, dripping blood, she swooped on to the small fat hiker and fastened her fingers round his throat.

'Stop! Ugh! Guggle!' gulped the small fat hiker.

'I know who you are,' she screeched. 'You're Henry.'

'No, I'm not,' he spluttered. 'I'm not Henry. I'm Pete.'

Ham had stopped sneering, and backed away.

The demented bride passed straight through the hiker called Pete and swooped down on the other

67

one. 'Then *you're* Henry,' she screamed.

'No, I'm not, I'm not,' stammered the tall thin hiker, trying to beat her off. 'I'm Joe.'

Major Hardbottock now stepped forward. You could say a lot about him but not that he was a coward.

'Henry is *my* name,' he said.

The effect on the mad bride was electric. She flew at Major Hardbottock, she kicked out at him, her fingernails reached for his eyes.

'It was Henry who shot me,' she yelled. 'And you'll pay for it!'

Major Hardbottock was a strong man but he had no chance against the demented spectre.

'I didn't, it wasn't me! I'm a different Henry,' he gasped, thrashing about wildly with his shooting stick.

'You have just seen another of Clawstone's famous ghosts,' said Mrs Grove, as the party stumbled away from the steam and the mingled smell of washing powder and blood. 'The Bloodstained Bride who was shot by her lover on her wedding day . . .' She told them Brenda's tragic story. 'It is most unfortunate,' she went on, 'that Major Hardbottock has the same name as the man who killed her.'

Actually, the name of the man who had shot Brenda had not been Henry, it had been Roderick, but as the visitors waited to buy tickets, Ned had recognized Henry Hardbottock from the telly. He had told the ghosts about him and Brenda had seen at once how she could make her haunt more interesting.

'I want to get out,' said Ham. 'Where's the exit?'

But Mrs Grove did not seem to have heard him. She had opened a door labelled 'Museum', and the cowed visitors shuffled in after her.

Inside the room, everything was quiet. The stuffed duck that had choked on a stickleback, the rocking horse with a missing leg, the cardboard gas-mask case were all in place.

'I will leave you to look at the exhibits on your own,' said Mrs Grove. 'If you want any help, just ask the curator.'

She pointed to a man sitting in a chair by the window with his back to them.

The visitors did their best to be interested in the exhibits. They were pale and shaken – the hikers kept feeling their throats – but it looked as though the worst might be over. The professor made a note of the medieval moulding over the fireplace. Then she bent over the Clawstone Hoggart.

'I've never seen anything like this,' she said to her assistant. 'Go and ask the curator what it is.'

Angela went over to the window and cleared her throat.

'Excuse me,' she said. 'I wonder if you could help me . . .'

The man swivelled round in his chair.

'No,' he said in a throbbing voice, 'I cannot help you. But *you* must help *me*.'

And he stood up and slowly, button by button, he opened his shirt.

For a moment everyone in the room was silent as they took in the ghastly sight which met them. Then the screaming began – and the stampede to try to reach the door.

But the apparition with the unspeakable creature gnawing at his chest was quicker than they were.

'You must take my burden,' he cried, barring the door. 'You must take my rat. Take it, take it!' He lunged out at Major Hardbottock. 'You! You are strong. Pluck it from me. Take it by the tail and pull.'

'Get away from me,' shouted the Major. 'You're unclean!'

'Yes, I'm unclean but you must save me. Or you.' He turned to the professor. 'Snatch it from me. Free me from the rat!'

Ham retched and bent over a fire bucket. Everyone was backing away now but there was no escaping the phantom with the rat. He swooped through the cage of Interesting Stones and past the sewing machine which had belonged to Sir George's grandmother. He beseeched and implored and pleaded – he went down on his knees and threw his arms round the visitors' legs – and all the time the loathsome animal on his chest gnawed and crunched and chewed and clung.

Even when they found another door and stumbled down a flight of steps the visitors could still hear the maniacal voice. The little girls were clutching their parents, the hikers were deathly pale, the professor's assistant was crying. All they thought of was getting out of the castle: out . . . out . . . out . . .

In the hall, The Feet were still dancing. The visitors stumbled through them. The nurse had run off, leaving the old lady to manage on her own.

'Look, there's an attendant!' cried the professor. 'Perhaps she'll show us the way out.'

The visitors looked uncertainly at each other, but after a moment Major Hardbottock resolutely made his way towards the girl sitting quietly on a chair at the far side of the room.

'How do we get out?' he asked.

'Yes, out, out quickly. Show us the way out,' begged the rest of the party.

The girl on the chair smiled. It was a sweet smile and the terrified visitors were calmed for a moment.

'This way,' she said.

She lifted an arm and pointed. Then she gave a little sigh, her lovely midriff separated into two bloodied and jagged halves, and the top part of her floated softly, gently, up and up towards the ceiling, while her lower half, in beautiful embroidered trousers, still sat peacefully on the chair.

Upstairs in their hiding place, the children waited eagerly. As soon as Sunita had joined herself up again they were going to signal to Mrs Grove to lead the visitors out.

But something had gone wrong. Sunita's top half still floated high up among the chandeliers, her long hair seemed to blow in some unseen breeze, but she did not come down again. She circled the huge room; she looked down, bewildered. She was lost. She could not find her lower half.

'Oh!' Madlyn clutched her brother. This was awful. What if Sunita could never find the rest of herself ?

They stared up at the ceiling – and then, as she gazed down at them, they saw her give an unmistakable wink.

She hadn't really lost the rest of her; she was just pretending so as to make her trick more scary. But this last haunting had been too much for one of the visitors. There was a clatter as a stick fell to the floor; then a dreadful thump as a body hit the ground.

But it wasn't delicate Mrs Field who had fainted. It

was the man who had walked to the North Pole and bitten off his own finger; the man who had crossed the Sahara without a single camel.

It was Major Henry Hardbottock who lay unconscious on the floor.

Twelve

It was a terrible moment.

'Oh, the poor man; how dreadful,' said Aunt Emily, running out of her room. 'What if he gets concussion?'

'What if he sues us?' said Sir George. 'We'd be ruined.'

While they waited for the ambulance, and Mrs Grove let out the other visitors, every kind of dreadful thought ran through the heads of the people in the castle. If the Major was seriously hurt they would never dare to let in visitors again. It looked as though, after all their hard work, the first Open-Day-with-Ghosts had ended in disaster.

The ghosts, of course, started to blame themselves.

'Perhaps I shouldn't have strangled him so hard,' said Brenda, and Mr Smith was worried that he had stuck the wrong hand out of the oak chest.

'It sometimes bothers people, seeing those slivers of muscle on the bone. Slivers can be very unsettling.'

By the time the ambulance men came with a stretcher, Major Hardbottock had come round, but they insisted on taking him to hospital for scans and a check-up.

'You never know with head injuries,' said the first man, looking solemn.

'I don't like the look of his eyes,' said the second.

So the Major was driven away, and in the castle

they settled down anxiously to wait for news.

Sir George rang the hospital in the early afternoon, and again an hour later, and then once more, but no one could tell him anything. The Major was still having tests.

'If they've found something serious I shall never forgive myself,' said Aunt Emily.

Supper was a silent and a gloomy meal. But just as they were clearing it away, Ned came running in from the village to tell them what he had seen on the seven o'clock news.

'He was sitting up in bed – the Major – surrounded by journalists and telling them about this amazing castle he had seen absolutely chock-full of ghosts.'

And sure enough, the following morning what the Major had said was in all the newspapers, with a big picture of him and a smaller, smudgy one of Clawstone.

The day after that, the Major gave a lecture. But it was not the one he usually gave called 'My Journey to the North Pole,' and it was not the one called 'My Travels in the Sahara'. It was called 'My Adventures in the Most Haunted House in Britain'.

So, within a very few days, the number of visitors to Clawstone doubled and then trebled and then quadrupled. People came with troublesome children, hoping they would be frightened into good behaviour; groups of youths abandoned their computer games to come to Clawstone; and parties arrived from bowling clubs and cricket associations and unions of transport workers and cheesemakers and dentists.

What's more, the first visitors, who had left screaming, came back, bringing their friends. The hikers who had been nearly throttled by Brenda brought their companions from the Ramblers' Club; the professor came with a batch of students; the little girls persuaded their teacher to bring the whole class – and old Mrs Field brought her physiotherapist.

'I can't understand it,' said poor Aunt Emily. 'Do you think people *like* being frightened?'

They increased the number of Open Days to two a week, and then three; they could have filled the castle every day, but they didn't because they didn't want to exhaust the ghosts.

'They work so hard,' said Madlyn, 'it wouldn't be fair.'

The Feet had danced so energetically that they had developed ectoplasmic blisters on their big toes, and in between haunting they just crept into the Wendy house and slept and slept and slept.

'I wish there was something we could do for them,' said Rollo.

'Maybe we could wash them – they're always washing people's feet in the Bible,' said Madlyn.

But no one knew quite how to do this and anyway it seemed rather rude, so they left it. They had become very fond of The Feet. Having them was rather like having a dog who understood much more than people realized.

Knowing how useful they had been made the phantoms really happy. After years of wandering they felt they had come home.

Being happy is good for people's health and this is as true of ghosts as of anyone. The rat became quieter; often it did not gnaw for hours at a time. Brenda shrieked less, and once, as they sat on the wall looking down on the park, she admitted that perhaps she had been a little unkind to Roderick, the man who had shot her.

'He was away in the war, you see, in Burma, and my mother said I must marry someone rich, so I accepted this man who made boots for the army.'

After the first week, Cousin Howard bicycled off to Greenwood to thank Mrs Lee-Perry and the ghosts at the Thursday Gatherings for their help, and they said it had been a pleasure.

'It's wonderful to know that dear George's cows will now be safe,' said Fifi Fenwick.

Because that, of course, was the point of it all. As the money came in – more and more of it – work began at once on the park. The walls were mended, the stream was dredged, the dead wood was cleared from the copses. Sir George walked with a spring in his step, and when cattle experts came from other countries he showed them round with pride.

'You'll see, my boy,' he said to Rollo, 'we'll have the finest herd in the world.'

'We have the finest herd now,' said Rollo.

Both George and Emily thanked the children most sincerely for what they had done and asked them if there was anything they wanted for themselves, but there wasn't; at least, not anything you could buy. Madlyn wanted her parents to come back and Rollo wanted to adopt a Siberian tiger in the zoo, but there was a waiting list.

'But I think you ought to buy yourself a new skirt,' said Madlyn to Aunt Emily.

'Oh, I couldn't do that, dear. I simply couldn't,' said Aunt Emily, looking shocked and worried. 'I've settled into this skirt; I wouldn't want to break in a new one, not at my age.'

But in the park the cattle lifted their heads proudly as if they knew that their future was secure. When Rollo went out now with the warden, Ned's uncle, in the trailer, he could identify all the animals. The two calves, who were friends and slept with their heads resting on each other's backs; the cow with the extra-long eyelashes, who stood for hours in the stream cooling her feet; the bullock who refused to fight but dozed the day away under his favourite willow tree . . .

Then one day Sir George came down from the roof with his telescope.

'There are more cars coming here than are going to Trembellow Towers,' he said.

He tried hard not to look pleased but he did not succeed. He looked very pleased indeed.

Thirteen

Lord Trembellow was in his new gravel pit, bullying his workmen, when Olive drew up in one of the Trembellow chauffeur-driven cars.

'Daddy, I've bad news,' she said. 'I've got yesterday's figures. Clawstone has beaten us by thirty-seven visitors. *Thirty-seven!*'

Her sallow face was even more pinched than usual; one could feel the awful numbers eating into her brain.

The gravel pit was a new one; Lord Trembellow had bought it two weeks earlier and already the Trembellow lorries were driving up in a steady stream, loading gravel, and reversing out again on to the road. There were great gashes in the hill sides; even after this short time hardly a blade of grass was to be seen. The noise of the diggers and the crushers and the earth movers was overwhelming; the air was full of dust and the smell of diesel fuel. It was Lord Trembellow's fifth gravel pit and the largest and the best.

'It'll be that rubbish about ghosts, I suppose,' he said now. 'Lies and trickery. Well, we'll get even with them. If they can get ghosts we can get ghosts. Bigger ghosts. Scarier ghosts. More of them.'

So that night he telephoned his son Neville in London and told him to buy some ghosts.

'I don't care what you pay,' he told Neville. 'Just get the best.'

But Neville said he didn't know how to buy ghosts, and anyway he was going up to Scotland to play golf.

'We'd better go ourselves, Daddy,' said Olive. 'Neville can be rather weak sometimes.'

So Lord Trembellow and his daughter decided to go to London. Lady Trembellow didn't want to come. Ever since she'd had her tummy tuck she'd felt ill and uncomfortable. It was the most expensive tummy tuck anyone had ever had, but it still hurt.

Before they left they made a shopping list.

'Nothing like lists to keep things tidy,' said Lord Trembellow. He picked up the local paper in which there was a description of the ghosts which haunted Clawstone. 'There's a Bloodstained Bride, it says here. So we'd better have one of them.'

'Why just one, Daddy? Why not two?' asked Olive, and she sat down and wrote:

'Bloodstained Brides: Two.'

'And a skeleton,' read out her father. 'Well, skeletons are common enough. We could have half a dozen.'

'Six skeletons,' wrote Olive.

'And there's this man with a rat,' read out Lord Trembellow. 'Ranulf de Torqueville, he's called.'

'We don't have to have just a *rat*,' said Olive. 'We could get something bigger. Or we could get *two* rats, one for the front and one for the back. And that girl who's sawn in half. Why only in half? Why not in quarters? Or in eighths? Eight pieces of girl . . .'

When they got to London they checked into the largest, glitziest hotel in the city and the next day they took a taxi to the largest, glitziest department store, where they bought two long satin wedding dresses and some jars of tomato ketchup. Then they went to a shop which supplied schools and hospitals with specimens for anatomy lessons, and bought half a dozen skeletons.

'The biggest you've got,' said Lord Trembellow.

After that they looked at rats in a pet shop but they were white and not suitable, so they got the address of a man who trained animals for films and television and he agreed to bring two stunt rats up to Trembellow. Hiring actors to pretend to be the ghosts was easy enough – actors are so often out of work that they will do anything for money – and a man who supplied circuses with their acts said he would try to send them a sawn-up girl.

'What about the Severed Feet?' asked Olive. 'We could ask in a hospital if they could spare any.'

But her father said they wouldn't bother. 'We've got enough here to scare the living daylights out of everyone.'

When they got back to Trembellow they got to work, but their preparations did not go smoothly. The actor who was supposed to be Ranulf de Torqueville took one look at the rats and fainted and they had to use inflatable rats instead. The two bloodstained brides hated each other on sight, and the sawn-in-half girl got tonsillitis and never turned up at all. To make up for this they ordered another dozen skeletons and got the most expensive computer firm they could find to set the skeletons dancing and leering and leaping out of cupboards.

'It'll be all right on the night,' said Lord Trembellow. 'It better be, after the money we've spent.'

But it wasn't. The actor who was pretending to be Ranulf was fond of jewellery and as he tore open his shirt, his uncut garnet ring caught on the front rat's rubber back, causing the animal to deflate with a sad squeak. As the visitors filed past the bloodstained brides, the first bride dug her elbows into her rival, who stumbled forward, causing the bottle of tomato ketchup she had hidden in her bra to fall out and spatter the white shoes of a Mrs Price from Barnsley, who was not amused.

Which left the skeletons. They began well, jumping and clacking and leering and gibbering – but the most expensive computer experts are not always the best. The skeletons danced faster and faster still – there was a high-pitched whining noise, then a whirring . . . and a jumble of tangled bones came crashing to the floor.

It was unfortunate that the bones were carefully labelled in blue ink for the schools who had ordered them for their studies. A skeleton labelled 'Property of St Oswald's College of Further Education' is not really a very frightening sight.

'I don't understand it,' said Lord Trembellow angrily when the visitors had gone off, jeering and scoffing. 'Why do the ghosts work at Clawstone and not here?'

Lady Trembellow was lying on the sofa with a hot water bottle on her stomach.

'Perhaps the Clawstone ghosts are real?' she suggested timidly.

'Don't be ridiculous, Phyllis,' snapped her husband.

It was time he sent her off for some more repair work, he thought. Maybe an implant on her lips to give her a bit of a pout. She still didn't look the way his wife should look.

As for Olive, she looked at her mother with contempt, because she always found it difficult to understand that she herself, who was so clever, had been born to a woman who was completely foolish. A woman who thought that ghosts could possibly exist.

Fourteen

It began like all the summer days at Clawstone since the coming of the ghosts. The children went up to the nursery to say good morning and then all of them went to sit on the wall and look across the park and plan their day.

This particular day promised to be an exceptionally beautiful one, with mist in the valley and a clear pale sky.

'I was a bit silly, buying wellington boots,' said Madlyn.

The cattle had become so used to the children that they grazed right under the wall or dozed in the shade of the overhanging elm. The youngest calf, the one that Rollo had seen being born, would look up and twitch his ears when Rollo called down to him.

'I'm sure I could tame him,' said Rollo, but he kept to his great-uncle's rule and did not go into the park alone. 'In any case they shouldn't be tamed,' he said. 'They have to be wild and free.'

Sunita, of course, could float down into the fields whenever she wanted to, and when she came the cattle just lifted their heads for a moment and went on grazing. Only the oldest cow, the one with the scars and the crumpled horn, limped after her and waited for a special word. The whole village seemed to share in the happiness of the castle. More visitors to the castle meant more visitors to the hotels and the pubs and the shops, but it wasn't just that. Ned had been right when he told Madlyn that the cattle who had been saved belonged to everyone.

But the ghosts never became smug. Before every Open Day they worked out new ways of scaring people, and now, though they would have liked to linger in the open air, the ghosts and the children made their way back to the castle for another run-through.

They were crossing the courtyard when a brown van drew up at the gate. Painted on the van were the words 'Veterinary Enterprises', and three men in white coats got out.

One was small, with a black, pointed beard, thick, black-rimmed glasses and a foxy face, and he wore a stethoscope round his neck.

The second one was tall and shambling with a sticking-out Adam's apple, and he carried a black bag like a doctor's.

The third man had been driving. He had slicked-down hair, full lips and highly polished shoes, and he was holding a clipboard.

Inside the van, as the doors opened, the children could see all sorts of instruments: syringes and coils of rubber tubing and thermometers and flasks.

The ghosts vanished. The children came closer.

'Good morning. Can we help you?' asked Madlyn politely.

'We want to see Sir George Percival,' said the foxy man, and he handed her a card which said 'Veterinary Enterprises (Northern Branch)'.

'I'll tell him.'

84

She ran off and returned with Sir George.

'I'm afraid you've come to the wrong place,' he said. 'We haven't called out any vets.'

The foxy man looked offended. 'My name is Dr Dale,' he said. 'And these are my assistants, Mr Blenkinsop and Mr French. We're from the Special Branch of the Ministry of Animal Health and we're doing a routine survey of farm animals in the area. It's part of a government initiative. You should have received a pamphlet.'

'Well, I haven't,' said Sir George shortly. He was not very fond of men from the ministry. 'Perhaps you had better speak to my warden, Mr Grove. He lives in the village.'

'We have already tried to contact Mr Grove. Apparently he's been taken ill; they suspect a diseased appendix, I'm told.'

Ned made a noise of surprise. 'I didn't know my uncle was ill,' he said.

The men in white coats ignored him.

'But we can perform the tests perfectly well without help. Indeed, we prefer to work alone. So if you will unlock the gates of the park . . . We shall only be here for a few hours.'

Sir George was not at all pleased. 'It would be very unwise for you to go into the park. The cattle are not usually vicious but if they are disturbed by strangers . . .'

Dr Dale smiled – a smug and knowing smile. 'We are quite familiar with animals of all sorts.'

He glanced at the pile of shiny instruments in the back of the van.

Rollo, standing next to his great-uncle, drew closer

and Sir George took his hand.

'I imagine you would like to see our authorization,' said Dr Dale.

'I certainly would.'

Dr Dale turned to the man with the slicked-down hair, who produced a whole sheaf of forms and papers, all stamped at the bottom with red letters and the initials 'VE' for 'Veterinary Enterprises'.

'Very well,' said Sir George reluctantly. 'But please understand that you go in at your own risk.'

'There's nothing to worry about, I assure you,' said Dr Dale. 'It's just a matter of taking blood tests and saliva samples and skin scrapings and getting them analysed in the laboratory. We do it every day. It's because of our work that the fine herds of this country are kept in perfect health.'

So Sir George, looking morose and angry, went ahead to unlock the gates, and the van disappeared up the track in search of the herd, who had moved on to the high ground by the waterfall.

The men were gone for a couple of hours. When they returned they were brief but reassuring. 'We should have the results in a couple of days. Our laboratory is in the south so we'll have to send the samples by special courier, but I'm sure we'll be able to give your fine animals a clean bill of health.'

And they drove off in their brown van.

'I'm sure it will be all right, dear,' said Aunt Emily, putting her hand on her brother's arm. 'Don't you remember when they tested the sheep at Greenwood for liver fluke and then they turned out to be perfectly all right?'

But Sir George only frowned.

'Where's the boy?' he said.

But Rollo had disappeared, and no one saw him for the rest of the day.

They tried to carry on as though nothing had happened. The ghosts worked harder than ever and came up with more and more ideas. Brenda had decided to swoop out of a picture in the banqueting hall. It was a painting of a lady with fair ringlets wearing a crinoline and she thought that when her face changed and she turned into a Bloodstained Bride it would give a very good effect. Mr Smith practised something he called 'The Somersault of Death' and The Feet had learned to dance a tango inside Sir George's riding boots.

But no one could quite hide their anxiety. Ned and his mother went to see his uncle in the cottage hospital. The warden had had bad stomach cramps and the doctors wouldn't let him go home till they found out what had caused them.

'I'm sure there's nothing wrong with the cattle,' he said, turning restlessly in his bed.

Everyone talked and worried about the men in white coats – everyone except Rollo. Rollo said nothing, and whenever anyone else mentioned them, he left the room. He hardly touched his food, and Madlyn spent her nights running to and from his bedroom because he cried out in his sleep.

And so two days passed, and then three days, and four – and on the fifth, the men returned.

'It's no good beating about the bush, sir,' said Dr Dale as soon as he got out of the van. 'The news is bad. We thought you'd like to see the results of the tests yourself. Here are the sputum figures. As you see, there's nine milligrams of pollutant per cc in all the animals tested. That's very indicative.' He pulled out another file. 'And these are the urine tests.' He paused while Sir George stared at the columns of figures. 'I'm afraid they don't leave any room for doubt. And the blood samples – well, you can see. With figures in the high forties we're in an area of serious infection.'

'And we noticed other symptoms. Lip smacking,' said the tall, gangling vet with the Adam's apple, 'and foot blistering.'

'No.' The cry came from Rollo. 'It isn't true.' The vets turned their back on him and addressed Sir George.

'But what ... what does it mean? What is the disease they have?'

The vets looked at him with sympathy. 'I'm afraid the figures can mean one thing and one thing only. Klappert's Disease.'

'Klappert's Disease?' Sir George was bewildered. 'I've never heard of it.'

'That's not surprising. The disease was first described by Klaus Klappert about ten years ago. We've been investigating it in secret ever since – there's a research station not far from here and I'm afraid –' he lowered his voice – 'a strain of the virus may have escaped. I can't tell you how dangerous it would be if the disease were to spread. The herds of Britain could be totally wiped out.'

'I don't believe it. Why my cattle?'

Dr Dale shrugged. 'These things happen. Perhaps it's the purity of the herd which has prevented resistance. I can see that it's a shock, but with swift and determined action we can restrict the damage in the area.'

'What kind of swift and determined action?' But he knew even before Dr Dale had spoken.

'The whole herd will have to be culled, sir. It's the law with this particular disease.'

'Culled' is a word which scientists use when they mean killed. Seal pups are culled when they are clubbed to death in their breeding grounds. Badgers are culled when they are gassed inside their setts.

Sir George was remembering the outbreak of foot-and-mouth disease some years ago. The government had ordered all the infected cattle to be killed and their bodies burned or buried. The animals were stunned with bolt guns and driven in lorries to the killing fields, or else shot where they stood. When the stench of burning flesh became too much for people to bear, the carcasses were buried in pits and covered in lime. The farms of England became a ghastly battlefield filled with smoke and the cries of people whose animals were doomed.

'It was like being in hell,' said Sir George.

Meanwhile, the vets said, there had to be the strictest quarantine. They took notices out of the van saying 'No Admittance' in red letters, and 'Quarantine' in yellow letters, and they gave instructions for ditches to be dug in front of every gate and troughs of disinfectant to be put there for people to dip their feet.

'Once the herd is culled and the fields have been fumigated you can allow people back again, but not till then. The whole area must be out of bounds.'

'You mean we can't have our Open Days?' asked Aunt Emily.

'Definitely not. That would be a sure way of spreading infection.'

But at the end, as they got back into the van, they were reassuring. 'Your beasts won't feel a moment of pain. From the moment they're stunned and fall to their knees it'll all be over for them. There's many a human being who would wish for such a painless death,' they said.

And then they drove away.

Fifteen

Sir George did not like picnics, and he particularly did not like picnics by the sea. He did not like sitting bolt upright in the sand, or paddling in icy water, or trudging across sand dunes carrying hampers and rugs.

But three days after the men in white coats had been, Sir George sat staring out to sea with his legs sticking out in front of him and his tweed hat jammed down on his head – and beside him sat his sister Emily. She too was not fond of picnics: her back hurt when she sat without a support and both the Percivals thought that folding chairs and beach umbrellas and those sorts of things were vulgar. Sir George wore his tweed suit and Emily wore her fifteen-year-old knitted skirt, and both of them wanted only one thing: that the picnic, and the day, should be over.

The bay where they sat was very beautiful: a golden curve of sand with a view of two islands in the distance, and just enough of a breeze to crown the waves with little crests of white. The tide was out; the hard-packed sand rippled near the waterline, the rocks sparkled in the sun. Madlyn and Ned had taken their nets and were fishing the pools, calling out to Rollo when they found a starfish or a scuttling crab or a cluster of anemones.

But Rollo, who could have named all the creatures

that they found, sat beside his Great-Uncle George, silent and still, as though he too was old, and had a back that hurt, and wished that the day was over.

The ghosts had stayed behind in the castle. They were going to keep Cousin Howard company.

'It's the salt spray from the sea, you know,' Ranulf had explained. 'A ghost's ectoplasm can stand most things, but salt makes it curdle.'

Actually this wasn't true. There is nothing that ghosts like better than a visit to the seaside, but the ghosts were being tactful. They thought that on this historic and horrible day, the family might like to be alone.

Madlyn had caught a tiny green fish with a frog-like face and called out to Rollo.

'Look! I think it's a blenny.'

Rollo glanced up for a moment, but he did not move from his great-uncle's side.

Madlyn bit her lip. 'I don't know what to do,' she said miserably to Ned. 'He can't go on like this.' She threw the fish back into the pool and pushed her hair out of her eyes.

'I don't want to spoil things for my parents, but perhaps I ought to ask them to come home.'

'He'll be better when today is past,' said Ned. 'He keeps seeing it all in his head.'

For this was the day when the men were coming to take away the cattle. It was to get Rollo out of the way that Sir George had insisted on this picnic by the sea.

'Come on, I'll take you for an ice cream,' Ned said to Madlyn. 'The van's just coming down.'

They came back with with three vanilla cones and handed one to Rollo who thanked them politely, but when they came back five minutes later he was still holding it out in front of him while the melting ice cream dripped down his hand.

And so the day dragged on.

They unpacked the lunch which Aunt Emily had prepared, and did their best with it. The eggs were not quite hard-boiled and squirted a little as they bit into them, the slices of cucumber inside the sandwiches seemed to be jet-propelled and shot on to their laps, and the scones were some that Emily had made for an earlier Open Day. But it didn't matter because quite soon everything they were eating became covered in sand.

In the afternoon, Madlyn and Ned found some children at the other end of the beach and joined them in a game of cricket – and then at last Uncle George took out his watch and said it was four o'clock and they could go home.

As they drove through the village there was no need to ask if it was all over. People stood outside their houses looking silent and grave, and when they waved to Sir George they might have been greeting a passing hearse.

And even through the windows of the car the children could smell what had happened. The summer scents which usually came on the breeze were gone: the smell of flowers, and fresh-cut grass, and heather from the hills. Instead there was only one odour: the heavy, dark stench of disinfectant, stinging the nostrils, catching the throat.

They got out and climbed stiffly up the steps. In the upstairs salon, the ghosts were waiting for them.

'We wanted to speak to you,' said Ranulf. He

93

looked tired and tense and under his shirt they could hear the rat greedily gnawing. 'We have come to a decision. We feel that we will be in the way if we stay. You will want to be private among yourselves.'

'With no Open Days you will not need us,' began Mr Smith, 'so we will go away and—'

What happened next surprised everyone and it surprised Madlyn most of all.

If there was one thing Madlyn was known for, it was her even temper, her good manners and her wish to behave well and make people happy. Now she suddenly went mad. She stamped her feet. She screamed. She hurled abuse.

'How dare you?' she yelled at the ghosts. 'I've had *enough*! Rollo's making himself ill – he'll probably die and my parents are miles away and I don't know what to do and now you *dare* to go away and leave us. I can't stand it, I can't and I won't—'

And she threw herself on to the ground and burst into violent and uncontrollable sobs.

The ghosts stood round in dismay. Aunt Emily tried to go to her and stepped back as Madlyn kicked out.

'Leave me alone. I hate you all. Just go away and leave me *alone*.'

And then, as they all stared helplessly, not knowing what to do, there was . . . a kind of stirring . . . and then, quite on their own, The Feet walked slowly, steadily, to where Madlyn lay on the ground, still shaken by sobs.

The Feet did not say anything, for reasons which are obvious, but they settled down to keep watch beside her. One foot guarded her left side, one foot guarded her right side – and what they were telling her was absolutely clear.

'We love you,' said The Feet, without uttering a single word. 'We will never leave you. We belong.'

That night Rollo ate his supper and went to bed quietly, and slept. Sometimes you have to grow up quickly – and the day on which the cattle left Clawstone was such a day.

Sixteen

The Trembellows were very pleased with themselves. They had done good to the countryside; they had helped the Ministry of Animal Health to make the farms of Britain safe – and they had made a tidy sum of money.

'Of course we could have got more, much more,' said Lord Trembellow now, spearing a piece of bacon. 'But I felt it was my duty to help those men.'

The family were having breakfast. Olive did not go to school – she was too clever to do lessons with ordinary children so she had a tutor who came in the afternoons – and Neville had come up from London.

'It's our best pit, Number Five,' said Neville. 'We could have got a fortune for the use of it.'

'Yes, we could, Daddy,' put in Olive.

'That's perfectly true, my little sugar plum,' said Lord Trembellow, wiping a dollop of marmalade from his chin. 'But sometimes one just wants to help. To do what is right and good.'

Lady Trembellow choked slightly on a corner of toast. She could not actually remember a single time when her husband had wanted to do what was right and good.

'We can easily manage with the other four pits,' said Lord Trembellow. 'It's only for three months and then Number Five will be in use again.'

'Not all of it, surely,' said Lady Trembellow. 'Not the part where the cattle are buried.'

'No, not that part, of course,' said Lord Trembellow impatiently. 'We would not want pieces of bone spoiling our gravel – the Trembellow gravel is famous for its purity. But Number Five is a very large pit. The waste ground at the back can be left undisturbed for a long time. And Dr Dale assured me that the carcasses would be buried with large amounts of lime and other chemicals. There'll hardly be a trace of the beasts left – not just the soft parts will be dissolved but the skeletons too, and then it'll be business as usual.'

Lord Trembellow took a sip of coffee and smiled at his family.

'It couldn't have worked out better,' he said.

The vets had put 'No Admittance' signs at the entrance to the gravel pit and shut off access from the road. Number Five would be a kind of Sleeping Beauty, sealed off from the world while the infected animals decomposed in the soil. Then in three months' time, Dr Dale had said, the Trembellow lorries could go in and out freely and the neighbourhood would be clean again.

But of course the real reason why Lord Trembellow was pleased was quite a different one.

Sir George's cattle were gone forever. Everyone said that the old man had given up – that he would not attempt to restock Clawstone. In any case, the beasts were the only ones of their kind in Britain. He was a broken man, according to the rumours – and with Clawstone in strict quarantine and no visitors allowed, he would not be able to earn money by having Open Days. All the Bloodstained Brides and Sawn-up

Girls wouldn't help him, thought Lord Trembellow gleefully, which meant that soon now, very soon, Sir George would sell him the park for building land. And at a much lower price than he would have asked before.

Those blasted cows had been in his way for too long, he thought. That they were rotting in his gravel pit made him feel good.

'Two hundred houses,' he murmured, seeing the park becoming useful at last.

Olive picked up her napkin and wiped her small pinched mouth.

'Two hundred and *fifty*, Daddy, don't you think?' she said.

Lady Trembellow said nothing. Her husband had arranged for her to have her ears operated on in London but she had a surprise for him. She wasn't going to have any more operations to make her look better. She didn't mind whether she looked better or not. What she wanted was to *feel* better, and to live a better life – and Trembellow Towers was not the place for that.

No one knew it yet – but Lady Trembellow was going away.

Seventeen

A great deal of nonsense has been written about banshees. In some books they're described as fairies, in others as witches or ghosts. They're supposed to be death portents, which means they appear when someone is about to die, but it could also mean that they look so awful that a person who sees them dies of shock, which is not the same at all. There are legends about banshees who wash out the bloodstained linen of the dead, and others about banshees who belong only to the royal families of Ireland.

But most books are agreed on one thing: banshees are very sorrowful and sad and what they do, if they possibly can, is *wail* – the proper kind of wailing which involves howling and weeping and the wringing of hands.

Banshees need to wail like footballers need to kick balls and opera singers need to sing and acrobats need to turn somersaults. If they don't get a chance to wail they seize up. But though they are strange and gloomy, and like dark places, banshees do not cheat. If they wail it is because there is something to wail *about* – and usually this means that somebody has died. But what sort of somebody? A banshee who is serious about her work isn't going to wail for some thugs who have hit each other on the head with broken bottles and landed in the local cemetery, or for a car thief who has smashed himself up going joyriding in a stolen car.

And as people became more and more unpleasant and slaughtered each other in stupid wars, banshees these days quite often found themselves wailing for animals.

The Johnston sisters were elderly and lived together in a small house in a quiet street in a London suburb and at first you might have thought they were exactly like so many old ladies who live together, bothering no one.

But if you looked carefully, you could see . . . signs. The sisters' eyes were slightly swollen and their noses were reddened at the tips from years of weeping, and there were bald patches on their scalps where they had pulled out tufts of grey hair in their grief.

There were other signs too: the collars of their black dresses often seemed to be damp and they drank enormous quantities of tea. To make tears, the body needs a lot of liquid – and there is nothing better for making tears than tea.

They were drinking tea now, sitting round the blue teapot with its knitted cosy, and dunking ginger biscuits, when they heard the newspapers dropping in through the letter box. There was the *Evening Herald*, the *Radio Times* – and the *Banshee Bulletin*.

And it was in the *Banshee Bulletin* that they saw an extraordinary piece of news.

'My goodness, how amazing!' said the eldest of the sisters. 'Who would have thought it?'

'Yes indeed,' said the middle sister. 'Quite extraordinary. And so sudden.'

100

'It's the last thing I would have expected,' said the youngest sister. She was delicate and took things hard.

There was a pause while they poured themselves another cup of tea. Then:

'You don't think . . . we ought to . . . ?' said the eldest sister.

'It makes one wonder, certainly,' said the middle sister.

The youngest sister swallowed the last of her biscuit. 'I haven't had a good wail for a long time. I feel quite bunged up. But it's a long way.'

'Yes, it's certainly a long way.'

'And we're not young any more.'

'No, we're definitely not young any more,' agreed the others.

There was another pause, during which more tea was drunk and ginger biscuits were dunked. Then: 'I do feel perhaps it's our duty to go,' said the eldest sister. 'Goodness knows what kind of banshees they have up in the north. They probably live in caves and wear skins.'

So the next morning the three ladies set off in their small black motor car. They had been careful not to clean the car because they wanted to merge into the background (banshees are very fond of merging) and they had packed it with food for the journey and rugs and a change of underclothes.

But the most important thing they took was an enormous cardboard box crammed full of clean and freshly ironed handkerchiefs, and this was sensible. A working banshee cannot have too many handkerchiefs – and the job they were going to do in

101

the distant north was one of the biggest they had ever taken on.

Rollo went on behaving well. Seeing Madlyn in such despair and anger had shaken him badly.

But he was not the same as he had been before. He was very quiet; no one heard him laugh; and he spent a lot of time with Sir George in his study, listening to stories of what it had been like to be a soldier in the war.

'You obeyed orders,' said Sir George. 'Sometimes it was very difficult and you thought the orders were wrong, but you obeyed them because you knew that the men who gave them were doing their duty. And it's the same now. The men who took the cattle were obeying orders from the government. They were doing their duty. When they killed the animals in the big foot-and-mouth outbreak in 2001, people screamed and threatened to shoot themselves, but making a fuss doesn't help. We have to obey orders and we have to do it quietly,' said the old man.

But when he was alone he would stand by the window, not moving, wondering if there was any point in going on.

It was a sad time everywhere. Cousin Howard went back to his library to see if he could find out something about the Hoggart – but, to tell the truth, he found researching Hoggarts a lot less interesting than helping to set up Open Days. Madlyn went down to Ned's bungalow and played computer games and tried to cheer up Ned's uncle, who had come out of hospital and blamed himself for not having noticed that there was something wrong with the cattle.

'I can't think why I didn't see it,' he said. 'They seemed just fine to me.'

The village too was quiet – a listless, sad quietness. And in the park the uncropped grass grew long, and longer; the roses in the hedges smelled of disinfectant; and it rained and rained and rained.

When the cattle had been gone for more than a week, Ranulf called the children up to the nursery.

'It's Sunita. She thinks there is something we should do,' said Ranulf. 'Go on, Sunita, you tell them.'

Sunita had been looking out of the window at the empty park. Now she turned and, though she spoke gently as she always did, they could see that what she was saying mattered to her very much.

'I think we should go and say goodbye to the cattle. I think we need to go and see the place where they are buried and wish their spirits a safe journey.'

'Pray over them, you mean?' asked Madlyn. 'Like a funeral service?'

'Well, yes . . . but not only like that.' She hesitated. 'In India cows are sacred because they provide milk and give their hides. But they're sacred too because . . .' She looked down, suddenly embarrassed. 'Because they carry the souls of the dead to heaven. They're sort of connected with heaven. In the old days people's bodies were sometimes taken for burial on the back of a bull or a cow to help them on their journey. I can't put it into words, but they're . . . special. And I don't think they should just be buried and forgotten without a ceremony.'

'A sort of leave-taking,' said Ned.

'Yes. And I think we wouldn't feel so wretched ourselves if this were done. Saying goodbye is

103

important.' She paused and looked at the children. 'What do you think?'

Rollo was the first to speak. 'Yes, of course,' he said firmly. 'We were silly not to do it before. We must go as soon as we can.'

Lord Trembellow had made no secret of the fact that the cattle were buried in his gravel pit: he was proud of helping the vets get rid of the infected beasts. But the pit was fifteen kilometres away, on the other side of the hill to Trembellow Towers.

'It's too far to walk there and back,' said Ned. 'But there's a bus one way at least. If the ghosts don't mind being invisible there shouldn't be any trouble.'

They decided to go on their own without saying anything to the grown-ups, and their chance came two days later when the Percivals were asked out to dinner with the Lord Lieutenant of the county, who lived in a mansion which was an hour's drive away from Clawstone. Both George and Emily hated going out to dinner, which meant changing out of their usual clothes and eating things which disagreed with them and staying up late.

But they went, and as soon as Uncle George's Bentley was out of sight, the children and the ghosts hurried down to the bus stop by the church.

The sun had gone down by the time they reached the road leading to pit Number Five. There were traffic cones in rows across the path, and a notice saying 'Out of Bounds' and another one saying 'No Admittance'.

When they got to the entrance to the pit itself, they found it roped off. The windows of the workmen's hut were boarded up. The hillside with its gashes looked threatening and sinister; flood water from the recent rains had collected into large puddles; old tin cans floated on the oil-stained water.

Rollo shivered and Madlyn looked at him anxiously. Had it been a mistake to come?

Certainly it made everything seem worse, seeing where those warm-blooded, lovely creatures had ended up.

The ghosts had glided on ahead. Sunita was looking very purposeful as she searched for the burial site. The Feet followed her, keeping close to her heels.

The rough track, with its churned mud and heavy wheel marks, veered round to the left and led into a wider piece of waste ground.

'There,' said Ranulf. 'That will be where they're buried.'

They had come to a large patch of flat ground, covered with recently turned-over earth. Diggers and crushers stood nearby, like great dinosaurs.

Sunita nodded. 'Yes. This must be the place.'

She began to move backwards and forwards over the burial site. Her arms were stretched out, her head was bent intently over the earth.

'It's strange,' she said after a few moments, 'I can't seem to—'

She broke off suddenly and clutched Brenda. The children drew closer to each other; the other ghosts took a step backwards.

'Oh heavens, what is it?' said Madlyn.

The pit had suddenly filled with the most appalling sounds . . . sounds like none they had heard before: horrible, troubling, somehow not decent.

First, a ghastly gurgling sort of grunt . . . Then a rasping, squawk-like screech . . . and lastly a kind of honking hoot which changed halfway into a croaking squeal.

'Who's there?' shouted Ned.

The noise stopped abruptly. The silence was absolute.

'Maybe it was an animal?' suggested Rollo.

But what kind of animal? And there had been more than one.

'I'm not going to let it stop me,' said Sunita. 'If it's werewolves, we can deal with them. They can't hurt ghosts.'

She began once more to glide round the patch of freshly dug earth, trying to make contact with the spirits of the creatures who lay below. Madlyn had brought a bunch of flowers; she held them in her hand, waiting till Sunita should give the signal and the ceremony begin.

But Sunita kept gliding steadily round the edge of the burial ground, then across it, and they could see that she was becoming troubled and uncertain.

'I don't understand it,' she murmured.

Five minutes passed, and then ten. It grew darker and colder, and Sunita became more and more bewildered and unsure.

Then the noise came again. It was louder than before, and even more horrible, and it died away in a hopeless kind of gurgling splutter.

And from behind a large digger there emerged . . . three grandmothers.

At least, they looked like grandmothers – the old-fashioned kind: plump, with grey hair and black clothes, and they carried not one handkerchief each but a whole bunch of them.

'Of course!' said Brenda. 'I know who you are. You're banshees.'

'Yes, of course we're banshees. And you're ghosts. But I can tell you this: whatever you're doing you're wasting your time,' said the eldest of the women.

'It's a disgrace,' said the middle one. 'We're going to complain when we get back – the *Banshee Bulletin* used to be a reliable newspaper but it seems it'll print any sort of rubbish nowadays. They don't check their facts. And poor Greta's in a dreadful state.'

'Yes, I am,' said the youngest. 'My insides are all knotted up and my throat's as curdled as custard.'

'People make a fuss about constipation, but it's nothing to what happens when a howl gets stuck inside you,' said the eldest banshee.

'We came three hundred miles to have a good wail and – well, you heard us,' said the middle one. 'If the Banshee Choral Society had been there, we'd have been struck off the register, making a noise like that.'

'But why? Why can't you wail?' asked Brenda, who felt herself close to these women.

'We can't wail because there's nothing to wail *about*.'

'There's nothing to wail *for*.'

'Wailing doesn't happen for nothing, you know. There has to be a reason.'

Sunita now glided closer to the women. She looked relieved, as though a weight had fallen off her shoulders.

'Yes, I see, I see,' she said. 'I couldn't understand it.

I thought I'd lost my power to connect. But they aren't here, are they?'

'You can say that again,' said the eldest banshee. 'There's nothing under that earth except more earth and more earth still.'

Rollo had stepped forward; he was trembling with excitement. 'You mean they aren't dead?'

The banshees shrugged. 'As to that, we couldn't say. But they aren't *here* and that's for sure.'

Eighteen

They had forced open the door of the workmen's hut and the banshees were making tea.

It was a crush with all of them inside – unlike the ghosts, the banshees were solid – but the fug was cosy. They had missed the last bus back to Clawstone, but the banshees had offered to drop them off on their way home.

'I don't understand it,' said Ranulf yet again. 'Why say the cattle are buried here when they aren't? What is Lord Trembellow up to?'

'If it was Lord Trembellow,' said Mr Smith. 'He may have been had.'

But why?

No one could understand it. The Feet had climbed on to the eldest banshee's knee and refused to get down.

'I feel I've seen them somewhere before,' she said, patting the hairy toes.

'Yes, I feel the same,' said the middle sister. 'Somewhere where we went to do a job. A funeral, I suppose, but I can't think where.'

And the youngest sister nodded and said that she too felt that The Feet were familiar.

But Rollo could think of one thing only. The fate of the cattle.

'Where can they *be*?' he said again and again, and

Madlyn sighed because it seemed to her cruel that Rollo should once again be given hope. If the animals weren't buried here they would be buried somewhere else.

'All the same, it's really strange,' said Ned. 'Why pretend to bury them?'

They had searched the site, using their torches, but found nothing. After the torrential rain, any hoof marks or tracks there might have been would have been washed away.

The banshees sipped their tea. The fug in the hut increased.

'We need some more water for the kettle,' said the middle banshee.

'I'll get it,' said Rollo.

He took the kettle and went out to the tap at the back of the hut. Wedged behind the standpipe was a long thin metal object. He pulled it out and shone his torch on it. It seemed to be the nozzle of a spray-gun. Well, that didn't help much. The workmen had probably used it to spray paint on to the lorries.

Rollo sighed. If only he could find some real evidence – something to prove that the cattle had been here – but there was nothing.

He picked up the kettle and went back into the hut.

Sir George had been in bed for an hour when he heard a knock, and Rollo, in his pyjamas, put his head round the door.

'I have to speak to you,' he said.

'Good heavens, boy, it's the middle of the night!'

'Yes, I know. But it's terribly important.'

Sir George put on his bedside lamp. He had

110

indigestion after his dinner party, and a headache from the wine.

'Well, come on then. What is it?'

Rollo came and stood by the bed. 'We went to say goodbye to the cows,' he said, 'and they aren't there.'

Sir George roused himself. 'You did what?'

So Rollo told him about the visit to the gravel pit. 'But Sunita couldn't get in touch with the spirits of the cows, and the banshees couldn't wail and that means that the cows aren't buried in the pit.'

Sir George looked at Rollo. The boy's face was lit up and excited, and he hated throwing cold water on his hopes.

'Look, Rollo, I have every respect for the ghosts. Ghosts are important and venerable. But they're ghosts. And banshees are banshees. They don't belong to the real world. The world where animals are infected and have to be buried safely and put away.'

'Sunita knows about the cattle. She *knows*. We have to find out what happened to them and where they are.'

Sir George sighed.

'Rollo, when we want something very much we will believe all sorts of things. You want to believe that the cattle are still alive and so do I, but—'

'They are alive. I know they are. They've been stolen and taken somewhere. I know. You should see my zoo magazine . . . animals are always being stolen.'

Sir George shook his head. 'What would be the point of stealing them? No one could get money for them – they're the only herd of white cattle in the country. They'd be recognized at once.'

But after he had sent Rollo back to bed he lay awake,

111

turning over what the boy had said. It was nonsense – of course it was nonsense. It was wishful thinking. Propped up on his pillows, Sir George remembered the D-Day landing. His best friend had been shot and fell beside him. Later, when there was a lull in the fighting, he went to the field station to see him and the doctor told him there was no hope, but George couldn't believe it.

'He's going to get better,' he kept saying. 'He's got a good colour.'

But the doctor was right. His comrade had died that night.

All the same, thought Sir George now, perhaps he would get in touch with the ministry and ask them to confirm the identity of the vets. And it might be a good idea to have a word with Lord Trembellow.

Rollo had gone to bed at last; all the children slept; the castle was silent.

But the ghosts were not asleep. As the clock struck midnight they glided one by one out of the nursery windows and set off along the road which led through the village.

No one saw them – they moved invisibly, and fast. At the first crossroads they separated. Ranulf and his rat went west, towards the hills and farms of the Lake District. Brenda took the road to the east, which led to the villages and resorts of the coast. Sunita and Mr Smith glided on till the road divided once again. Then Sunita and The Feet made their way southwards, heading for the big towns. Mr Smith went north.

They had said nothing to the children. A Ghost Search is best carried out silently and without witnesses – for the people that must be sought out and questioned are often shy of the undead; they will only help or speak to others of their own kind. And it was from phantoms like themselves that the ghosts of Clawstone hoped to discover what had happened to the cattle.

Ranulf's ancestors had come from the Lake District; the de Torquevilles had owned big tracts of land there; the wicked brother who had imprisoned Ranulf had been Sheriff of Westmorland. The roads that carried the traffic now were built on the tracks and lanes that Ranulf had known as a boy, and many of them were still steep and narrow. If a truck big enough to take a load of cattle wanted to get through, it would have to take the big motorway to Keswick. .

'Oh, do be quiet,' said Ranulf to the rat.

But the rodent sensed that they were returning to his home ground. He had been a lakeside rat, one of six who had moved to the ancestral home of the de Torquevilles, and he swooped up and down Ranulf 's chest as if he was on a skating rink.

Just before the road widened for the motorway there was a lay-by with picnic tables and litter bins. It was on this spot that Ranulf's old friend Marmaduke Franshaw had passed on and become a ghost. He had been practising with his longbow when there was a sudden thunderstorm, and Marmaduke, who should have known better, took shelter under a tree and was struck by lightning.

Ranulf and Marmaduke had shared a tutor, they had ridden together and courted the same girls. Marmaduke had been a keen sportsman, able to follow the spoor of any animal he was hunting. If anyone had noticed a large lorry carrying animals it would be him.

Ranulf sat down on a milestone and prepared to wait.

Sunita's first stop was in the town where the old ghost with head lice was living – the one who had been at the audition but decided to return to her friends. It had stuck in Sunita's mind that the old woman had said she lived in a bus shelter near the slaughterhouse.

The word 'slaughterhouse' made Sunita feel sick, but if there was any trafficking in stolen animals for slaughter she would have to look into it.

'No, can't say I've noticed anything,' said the old woman when Sunita had tracked her down. She bent over a brazier to stir something in a pot, and Sunita saw the lice, silver in the moonlight, drop one by one into the stew. 'It's not used now, the slaughterhouse; it's all locked up. I'd have noticed if anything had come in. They make an awful din, these great lorries – like trains they are, with iron cages and all. Nasty things.'

Beside Sunita, The Feet stirred restlessly. They did not *think* being opposite a slaughterhouse with an old lady who dripped lice was bad for Sunita; they did not think anything at all – but they felt it through the skin of their toes and the soles of their feet and they moved closer to Sunita.

'Fond of you, aren't they?' said the old lady, looking down at them.

She beckoned to some of the other ghosts who lived rough, but no one had seen anything, and Sunita and

The Feet went on wearily gliding south. It was going to be a long night.

The first ghost whom Brenda met as she glided east to the seaside was Fifi Fenwick, exercising her bull terriers. Phantom dogs are usually black, but Fifi's bull terriers had stayed the same colour they were when they were alive – white with an occasional brown ear – so Brenda saw them at once.

Fifi was immensely interested, of course, to hear that the cattle were not buried where they were supposed to be, and very anxious to help, but she had seen nothing.

'I mostly stay on the beach,' she said. 'It's easier for the dogs. But I'll tell everyone at the Thursday Gatherings, of course – they may have heard something. Those lorries make a devilish noise – even when they drive at night they shake the windows.'

She asked after Brenda's mother and was sorry to hear that she had not become a ghost but stayed where she was, underground.

'You'll miss her,' she said, and Brenda agreed that she missed her badly.

'Though of course if she hadn't made me marry the boot manufacturer, Roderick wouldn't have shot me, and Mummy and I would have been together longer.'

'There's a big garage on the way to Seahouses,' said Fifi. 'It's open all night and they're doing a road survey there. Something about widening the road. They might be able to help you.'

And she called her dogs to heel and strode off up the beach.

*

Mr Smith, like all men who have made their living by driving taxis, had a very good sense of direction. He could see the roads between England and Scotland in his head as clearly as he had seen the veins on his hand when he still had proper hands. And of the three main roads that led north over the border, the most likely one for a heavy vehicle to take was the road on the flat plain between the coast and the Lammermuir hills.

And as luck would have it, it was there that an old friend of his, who had given up taxis and become a lorry driver, had met with a fatal accident.

Hal Striver had gone head-on into an outsize transporter which had skidded on black ice – one of those juggernauts that should not have been on the road at all – and since then Hal had haunted the garage and the transport cafe near the site of the accident.

He was quite a well-known ghost, not particularly shy, and drivers eating their egg and chips often saw him wandering between the tables. But what Hal mostly did was watch the traffic – he'd been on the roads all his life and to him cars and lorries had personalities, like people. And when he saw a juggernaut, the kind that killed him, he would clench his fists and call rude words after the retreating lorry.

Mr Smith saw him at once. He was standing in the forecourt of the garage, staring at the road, and he hadn't changed at all. He still wore the blue overalls he had worn when he was driving, and the flat cap, and for a moment Mr Smith was worried because, of course, he himself had changed tremendously.

And at first Hal looked very surprised to see a skeleton coming towards him, but as soon as Mr

Smith greeted him, his face lit up. 'Well, well, Doug, old man, it's good to see you.' He looked his friend up and down. 'What have you been up to? Lost a lot of weight,' said Hal, and burst out laughing. 'Never thought you'd end up a skeleton. Remember how we all teased you because you were too fat to get into the cab?'

They talked about the old days for a while but then Mr Smith came to the point. 'I need your help, Hal,' he said. 'I'm looking for a big truck – perhaps two – carrying a load of cattle. Would have gone through sometime in the last week.'

'Are you, then?' said Hal thoughtfully. He lifted his cap and scratched his head. 'Now let me see . . .'

In Cousin Howard's library the children waited. They had been there most of the day, since they woke to find the nursery empty.

There had been no time to panic – Cousin Howard had given them the message which the ghosts had left as soon they woke – but the waiting was hard. They had never known time go so slowly.

Then, in the early afternoon, Sunita came in through the window, carrying The Feet. Both of them looked utterly exhausted and even before Sunita shook her head they realized that there was no news.

Brenda came in soon after that. Her veil was tangled and her bullet holes had dried out on the long journey.

'Nothing,' she said wearily. 'No one's seen anything.' Ranulf came next. His shirt had blown open and they could see the weary rat lying like a limp dishcloth against his chest.

117

Ranulf did not speak; he only shook his head and collapsed on to the couch.

It was hopeless, then. Dead or alive, the cattle were gone.

Mr Smith came last. He too was exhausted. As he touched the floor his leg bones seemed to give way under him and for a few moments he could not get his breath. But when he roused himself they saw that his single eye was shining, and his skull looked as though it was lit up from within.

'I have news,' he said. 'There has been a sighting. All is not lost!'

And he told them what he had discovered.

'I've got this friend, Hal Striver,' Mr Smith began, 'and there's nothing he doesn't know about motor transport. Well, last week – on Thursday night it was – he saw two big cattle trucks pull up by the garage, and one of the drivers got out and went into the cafe but he didn't stay more than a minute, and no one else got out. So Hal went to have a look and he saw it was chock-full of cattle, but the animals were very quiet – he thought they must have been drugged. They often drug animals now when they move them. Anyway, Hal had a look inside the cab of the driver who'd got out, and he saw a map on the dashboard and a ring round one particular place.'

Mr Smith paused and the children waited, trying desperately not to show their impatience.

'Hal reckons he knows where the cattle were going. To a place called Blackscar Island. It's over the border, in Scotland, off the north-east coast, and it's a funny place, Hal said. There's a causeway you can drive over at low tide, but at high tide the island's completely cut off. No one knows much about it because it's so isolated and the people who own it don't like visitors, but Hal reckons he's seen other loads bound for there.'

'And it was last Thursday night that he saw them?' asked Ned.

Mr Smith nodded. 'The night after the cattle were taken from here.'

'Did he see what colour they were?' asked Madlyn.

'No. It was dark and there were only small gaps in between the slats. But he did say he thought they were horned.'

'I don't understand it,' said Sunita. 'Why pretend to bury the cattle and then take them somewhere else?'

No one could understand it. 'It doesn't matter whether we understand it or not,' said Rollo. 'We shall find out when we get there.'

'Get where?' said Madlyn – though she knew, of course.

'To this island place. To Blackscar.'

Nineteen

It would have been all right, thought Madlyn; she would have been able to hold Rollo back, but everything was against her. First of all Sir George came down to breakfast in his suit, which was only twenty years old, instead of in his thirty-year-old ginger tweeds, and said he was going to London.

He didn't tell the children why he was going but he looked worried and preoccupied. The truth was that he had decided to go to the Ministry of Animal Health and find out more about the disease which had felled his cattle.

Then Aunt Emily, after staggering about bravely with her eyes half closed against the light, went to bed with one of her sick headaches.

'You will be all right, won't you?' she said anxiously to Madlyn. 'Mrs Grove will come up if you want her to.'

'We'll be perfectly all right,' said Madlyn firmly.

The last bit of bad luck for Madlyn was that Mrs Grove, not knowing that Emily was laid up, took a local train to Berwick to visit her brother, who had left hospital and was staying with a friend.

Nothing could stop Rollo now.

'We have to go to Blackscar. We have to see what's happened.' It was no good trying to get him to see sense; no good telling him that the animals that Hal had seen could have been any load of cattle going to any slaughterhouse in the country. He was like a zombie. 'We have to go,' he kept repeating. 'We have to.'

'How?' said Madlyn angrily. 'How do you think you can get to this Blackscar place. It's over a hundred miles away, over the border.'

'We can drive,' said Rollo.

'Oh we can, can we? And who's going to drive us?'

'I can drive,' said Ned unexpectedly. 'My uncle lets me drive his estate car in the park.'

Madlyn glared at him. Ned was usually on her side; she had learned to rely on him.

'Oh yes? And you've got a licence, I suppose, at your age.'

Ned shrugged. 'I didn't say I had a licence. I said I could drive.'

'And get arrested as soon as the first police car sees us. You're mad.'

Rollo turned to Mr Smith.

'You can drive,' he said. 'You must be able to. You were a taxi driver.'

'I may have been a taxi driver once, but I'm a skeleton now,' said Mr Smith.

'But you could, if you had to, couldn't you?' Rollo went on.

The skeleton sighed, 'You've no idea how much ectoplasmic force it takes to move things when you've passed on,' he said. 'Look at Brenda – she always has to rest after she's strangled someone. It isn't as though we're poltergeists.'

'No indeed, we are definitely not poltergeists,' agreed Ranulf, sounding quite shocked. 'Poltergeists

121

are just vulgar bundles of force.'

'And nasty bundles at that,' said Brenda. 'Bang, crash, thump! No skill. No care for other people.'

'Well, then it'll have to be Ned,' said Rollo.

'No!' said Madlyn. 'I won't have Ned sent to prison or wherever they send children to. If I have to choose between being driven by a skeleton or an eleven-year-old boy, I'd rather it was a skeleton. But anyway, we haven't got anything to drive in so there's no point in arguing. Uncle George has taken his Bentley.'

'There's my uncle's estate,' said Ned. 'He hasn't used it since he came out of hospital. It's old but it goes.'

In the end the skeleton and the boy took turns to drive the ancient, rattling car up to the Scottish border, towards the flat, low-lying eastern shore. Ned had filled the tank from the petrol pump in the farmyard and when Madlyn saw that she couldn't stop them going, she knew she had to come too – and she packed a hamper of food and some warm clothes and their toothbrushes. If Rollo was killed by a cattle rustler at least he'd die with clean teeth.

They had waited till it was dark. Mr Smith wore his overcoat with the hood up and no one stopped him, but it was a nightmare journey. He'd been the safest of drivers when he was alive, but now his finger bones slipped on the steering wheel and his single eye gave him distorted vision. Nor was it any better when Ned drove: his legs were really too short to reach the pedals, and his gear changes made Mr Smith wince.

In the back, the ghosts sent out waves of ectoplasmic force to help but it wasn't easy. Ranulf's rat was gagging badly: rodents are good on ships but motor transport doesn't agree with them. And being in a car always reminded Brenda of the drive to church for her wedding and made her weepy.

But somehow they did it. The journey, which should have taken two hours, took nearly four, but well before dawn they saw the outlines of the Lammermuir hills to the west. Their headlights caught fields of sheep, copses, an occasional farmhouse, but it was a bleak and empty landscape that they were coming to.

Then, still before sunrise, they reached the sea and saw before them a low dark shape in the water.

They had arrived.

The tide was high. They could hear the water lapping on the rocks. It would be several hours before they could hope to get across to the island. What they needed now was somewhere to sleep.

'I've never seen such a lonely place,' said Madlyn. 'There doesn't seem to be anyone living here at all.'

There was no sign of a village or even a farmhouse – but standing quite by itself on a spit of land was a church.

It was a very small church, and very simple, but solid and well built to withstand the winds from the sea. It was too dark to make out more than the outline: the squat tower, the arched windows. Surrounding it was a small graveyard. The building looked almost like the turf from which it sprang.

The children walked slowly up to the big wooden door.

'It'll be locked,' said Ned. 'They always are these days.'

123

But it was not locked. The door drew back, creaking, and they were in the dim interior. A few brass plates reflected what little light there was, but the inside of the church was as simple as the outside. There was a row of pews with flat cushions; the windows were filled with plain glass.

'Could we sleep here?' wondered Madlyn. 'Or would it be disrespectful to God?'

'People have always sheltered in churches,' said Ned. 'It's called seeking sanctuary.'

'Yes, I know, people . . . but ghosts?'

'It should be all right if they haven't been wicked.'

But they weren't sure. Sinners are always welcome in a church or any House of God as long as they have repented – but what if they haven't? It would be so embarrassing if there were thunderclaps or bolts from heaven when their friends tried to come in.

'We'll stay outside,' said Ranulf. 'Ghosts can rest anywhere.'

But the children felt it would be rude to go inside and leave their companions out in the cold.

So Ranulf glided across the porch and into the church and there were absolutely no thunderbolts of any kind. Obviously Ranulf had not been wicked and nor had the rat. (Gnawing is not wicked if you are a rat because gnawing is what rats *do*.) Mr Smith too passed peacefully into the church, and so did Sunita.

They were a bit worried about Brenda, because she had broken her promise to Roderick when she married the boot manufacturer, but breaking promises, though bad, is so common that it isn't really a sin and she got in too and flopped down on a pew.

124

Then Sunita turned to The Feet, which were standing outside on the porch.

'Come along, dears,' she said to them.

But The Feet didn't come along, even for Sunita. The Feet absolutely wouldn't enter the church; they wouldn't even try. They turned away firmly and the children could just make out the heels disappearing in the direction of a tombstone before the darkness swallowed them completely.

'Oh well,' said Madlyn. 'Perhaps they just want to be alone.'

They were all too tired to argue, and one by one they stretched out on the pews and went to sleep.

And while they slept, the water receded and Blackscar began to lift itself out of the morning mist.

It was called Blackscar Island but it was only an island part of the time. The causeway built across the sands could carry cars and people from the mainland, but it was only passable at low tide and for a few hours on either side of it. At high tide Blackscar was as complete an island as any in the North Sea.

Because of this there had been talk among seafarers in the olden days of people, or flocks of sheep, walking on the water . . . and miracles – but they were walking on the submerged causeway. And anyone who set off later than the time shown on the noticeboards on either side of the causeway risked drowning. There was a list of those who had perished in this way in the church, and to prevent further accidents a kind of wooden hut on stilts had been built halfway across, with a ladder leading up to it, where foolish travellers could take refuge till the tide turned again.

It was called the Blackscar Box and was not at all a comfortable place in which to spend the night.

The coast near Blackscar is bleak: flat and muddy with reeds and sandbanks – the island stretches a drear arm out into the grey water. All the same, years earlier a property developer had decided to build a luxury hotel on it. He thought people might be excited by the difficulty of getting across to the island, and by the loneliness.

The hotel he built was very grand: it had towers and turrets, and glassed verandas attached to each of the bedrooms. It had a palm court, where visiting orchestras could play, and three lounges, and the bathrooms had shell-shaped baths with gold-plated taps.

And at first people did come and the hotel did good business.

But the weather was terrible: fogs and wind and endlessly grey skies. The birds whose sad cries kept the visitors awake were not the kind that rich people liked to shoot, and the fish were just . . . fish – not the sort you could be photographed with when you had caught them. Who wants to be photographed with a herring?

And then a very important visitor ignored the noticeboard telling him the times of the high tide, and was drowned in his expensive motor car, and fewer and fewer visitors came, and the hotel went bankrupt.

The hotel stayed empty for nearly ten years. Then a very important doctor from London came and bought it – and with the hotel went the whole island: the fields and the marshes and the foreshore.

The name of the doctor was Maurice Manners and he was a man with a dream.

Dr Manners moved into the main part of the hotel – in fact he made it even grander – but the part where the servants used to sleep he turned into workshops and offices. He built wooden huts on the far side of the hotel and large sheds, and he fenced off paddocks, and he brought in like-minded people to help him with his business.

But exactly what his business was, no one knew, because visitors were not welcome at Blackscar. Dr Manners needed peace and solitude for his work, and for a long time now only those who had been specially invited made the crossing to the island.

Rollo woke first, and came out of the chapel to see the silver ribbon of the sea-washed road disappearing into the morning mist.

He would have set off then and there but Madlyn made them all eat some bread and butter and wash as best they could under the tap they found in the vestry. They had parked the car behind the church; with luck no one had seen it from the island, and they could make their way across on foot without being noticed.

'We've got to hurry,' Rollo kept saying, 'before everybody wakes up.'

The ghosts meant to come with them but they were having trouble with The Feet. The Feet had spent the night on a moss-covered tombstone at the edge of the churchyard. It didn't seem to be so different from any of the other tombstones – slightly crooked, with crumbling stonework and a name carved into it which was difficult to read. The name on this particular tombstone was ISH, which was unusual, but this was the place where The Feet wanted to be, and when it was time to set off for the island they refused to move.

Even Sunita couldn't make them come away. When she called them, The Feet would take a few steps towards her and then they would sort of fall in on themselves, the toes curled under, and, even in the cold of early morning, a sweat broke out on their skin.

'We'll catch you up,' said Ranulf, and the children scrambled down on to the sands and set off along the causeway.

It was easy to believe that only an hour earlier the road that they walked on had been under water; there were still puddles between the uneven stones. On either side of them, on the sands, waders and oystercatchers were looking for shellfish left in the shallow pools. The receding water sucked and eddied round the wooden piles.

Halfway across, they passed the ladder leading to the Blackscar Box; but they kept steadily on. They could only hope that the mist was hiding them from the windows of the hotel. Fortunately the hotel had been built so as to face away from the mainland, with most of the windows looking out on the open sea.

When they reached the island itself they left the causeway and dropped down on to the foreshore, seeking the shelter of the dunes, crawling through the marram grass and between hummocks of sand.

So far they had met nobody.

Every so often they made their way to the top of a dune and looked out on the interior of the island. They could make out the ornate building of the hotel, a row of wooden huts and a big windowless building almost the size of an aircraft hangar.

They had come to a small bay with a wooden jetty. The water here was deep and would provide good anchorage for seagoing boats, but there were no boats to be seen. Running across the gravelly sand, they found that the foreshore on the far side of the bay had levelled out; the dunes were less steep. An upturned rowing boat gave them a hiding place from which to watch.

Smoke was coming out of the chimney of one of the huts, but still nobody seemed to be about.

And then they heard a sound that stopped them dead in their tracks. A low mooing, followed by silence. Then the same sound, repeated.

There was no holding Rollo back now; the others did not even try. He broke cover and raced across the turf towards the noise they had heard, and they went with him.

They came to a high wooden fence, topped by an electric wire. Running round the fence, they reached a gate through which they could see into the paddock.

And in the paddock was a herd of cattle.

The three children stood absolutely still. Oddly, it was Madlyn, not Rollo, who had to blink back tears. Rollo's disappointment was so great that he could only stare in silence, holding on to the wooden bars of the gate.

For while it was true that the field was full of cattle – cows and bulls and calves – these were not the Wild White Cattle of Clawstone that they had come so far to seek. The pelts of these beasts did not take the light; their hides were dull and lifeless. There was hay in the paddock, and troughs of water, but the animals were not feeding. They lay listlessly, like dark hummocks, on the trampled grass.

And they were brown. Every single animal was a dark and uniform brown.

The children stood there, completely winded. They had come all this way for nothing. Ned was the first to pull himself together.

'Well, that's it then,' he said. 'We'd better get out before we're caught.'

But Rollo did not move. He was staring at the beasts and breathing hard.

No,' he said. 'Wait.' And then: 'Look – look at that calf over by the trough.'

'What about it ?' said Madlyn.

'Look at the way it's butting its head. And over there – the old cow up against the fence. Look at her horn.'

The others looked, but at first they did not understand.

'Look at her horn,' repeated Rollo.

'It's crumpled,' said Madlyn under her breath.

Then the great bull, who had been lying down, half hidden by the other beasts, got suddenly to his feet and now they all saw what Rollo saw. For, brown or not, this was the great king bull of Clawstone.

The ghosts had caught up now, and above them they heard Sunita's voice.

'What have they done?' she breathed in horror.

It was now that they remembered the nozzle of the spray-gun in the gravel pit. The cows must have been to the pit, then, and sprayed . . . but why? So that they could be stolen and carried off to another part of the

130

country? Stolen from the vets who were going to bury them, so that they could be sold perhaps for slaughter in some place where people did not care whether the animals were infected or not?

Why should anyone disguise the cows unless they were doing something illegal, and meant them harm?

But Madlyn had had enough.

'We're going to go back now and tell Uncle George and the police about this. And quickly.' They turned and ran back, dropping down on to the sands again, trudging through piles of seaweed, skirting the rock pools. The wind was freshening, blowing from the north. They crossed the bay with the jetty safely; they were nearly there. It was only a short run across the beach to the causeway. 'Stop!'

The voice was deep, foreign. Barring the way was a man wearing baggy trousers and an embroidered tunic. His face was sunburned, he had a large curving moustache and he carried a pitchfork. For a moment the children thought they might be able to run for it – but now a second man, with an even larger moustache and even baggier trousers, appeared from behind a bush, armed with a heavy stick. They did not look like the kind of people from whom it would be easy to escape.

'You come with us,' said the first man. 'Now. Quick. The boss, he waits.'

And the children were led away.

Twenty

It was easy to see that the building they were taken to had been a hotel – and not an ordinary hotel: a hotel for people who had been very rich indeed.

As the children were led along a corridor their feet sank into deep-pile carpets; there were chandeliers instead of ordinary lamps; hot air came up through vents in the walls, and the fireplaces were made of marble. It was extraordinary, finding all this luxury while outside lay the bleak island with its wind-flattened grass.

And floating invisibly above the children were the ghosts.

The men with baggy trousers did not seem to be allowed in the hotel. They had pushed the children inside and it was a large, muscular woman in a maid's uniform who led them up the wide staircase and knocked on a door with a brass plate on it saying 'Dr Maurice Manners M.B.B.S. M.R.C.G.P.'

A voice said, 'Come in,' and they were pushed forward into the study of the man who owned the island.

Dr Manners sat behind an enormous desk on which was a bust of the great naturalist Charles Darwin. Although it was early in the morning, he was formally dressed in a pale grey suit with a mauve silk shirt and matching tie. He had fair wavy hair lightly touched with silver at the temples, and his hands, with their long fingers and beautifully manicured nails, were folded over a neat sheaf of papers on his desk. The sweet smell of toilet water, which he had mixed for him specially, hung over the room.

When he saw the children he smiled – a warm, friendly smile.

'Well, well,' he said. 'You're very early. You've come to thank me, I imagine, but there was no need. I don't require praise. What I do, I do for the satisfaction of a job well done.'

All three children gaped at him. Madlyn was the first to find her voice.

'You stole our cows – the Clawstone cattle. You needn't think we didn't recognize them just because they were dyed.'

Dr Manners's smile grew even more charming.

'You could say I stole them. But I prefer the word "rescue".'

'What do you mean?' said Madlyn. 'I don't understand.'

'It's quite simple. Your cows were under sentence of death, were they not? They were due to be killed?'

'Yes.' Rollo had found his voice. 'They had Klappert's Disease.'

'Exactly so. The vets from the ministry found that they had this disease and the vets were perfectly correct. People like that don't make a mistake.' He pressed the tips of his fingers together. 'And the regulations say that animals infected in this way must be destroyed instantly and the carcasses buried. That is the law and the law must be obeyed, must it not?'

'Yes.' All three children nodded their heads.

'But to kill animals unnecessarily is a sin. To kill at all, except in self-defence, is wicked. At least that is what I believe.'

'It is what we believe too,' said Ned.

'Good. Good.' Again he smiled that very charming smile. 'Not everybody can act on their beliefs, of course. However, I am fortunate in that I can.' He glanced out of the window at a group of men who were going past. Some wore white coats, some were in overalls – all of them looked purposeful and busy. 'I have helpers, you see. Marvellous helpers for whom I give thanks every day of my life. I have scientists trained in all the problems of animal health. And not only scientists.' He leaned across to the children. 'I wonder if you have ever heard of a country called Mundania?'

The children shook their heads.

'It is a beautiful place, high in the mountains of central Europe. The people who live there are strong and fearless – but noble too – and when they heard rumours of my mission they came of their own free will to work for me.'

'Are those the people who brought us here?' asked Ned.

'They are.'

'But I still don't understand what happened to our cattle,' said Rollo. 'I still don't understand what it is that you do.'

'No, I dare say you don't. My work is unusual – but I will try to explain. As you know, your cows have Klappert's Disease, and animals with Klappert's must be killed immediately. But suppose there is an antidote. Suppose there is something that can remove the diseased cells in the blood? Suppose there is a treatment that will cure the animals, wouldn't you think that they should have it?'

'Yes. Yes, of course.'

Dr Manners leaned back in his chair. A shaft of light fell on his golden head.

'And there is such a treatment,' he said softly. 'We have found it here, and developed it in our laboratories. There is a vaccine but it is very, very expensive – and no government will ever pay out money if it doesn't have to. We tried to convince them, of course, but they refused to listen – they didn't believe in our results. Killing the animals was quicker and more economical. So we have had to act outside the law. You see, the vets from the ministry don't actually kill and bury the animals themselves; they give that work to other people. It's called outsourcing – you may have heard of it. And sometimes they give that work to me and my assistants. They think we are a slaughtering company but actually, secretly, we are quite the opposite. We are the Manners Save the Animals Mission – SAM for short.'

He got up and went over to the window.

'So we took the cattle to the gravel pit – they'd been stunned with anaesthetic darts in the field – and officially we buried them so that the trail went cold. But in fact we dyed them so that they would not be recognized, and brought them here. As far as the men from the ministry were concerned, the cattle were dead and buried. It was over. But for your beautiful beasts,' he said, turning back to the children, 'for the famous Wild White Cattle of Clawstone, a new life has begun. Because soon now – very soon – perhaps even tonight,' said Dr Manners, and his high voice rang out across the room, 'a boat will come. A boat which will carry them to a far country where they can graze in peace till the end of their lives . . . to a park with shady trees and wonderful flowers and sparkling streams . . .'

'Where?' asked Madlyn. 'Where is there such a park?'

Dr Manners shook his head. 'That I cannot tell you. There is always a danger that they would be found and brought back and slaughtered – slaughtered unnecessarily like so many animals in this cruel, harsh world. But I swear that the place they are going to is as close as you can get to paradise on earth.' He looked down and his expression, as his eyes fell on Rollo, was very kind. 'I know how hard it is to let go of creatures that you have grown to love,' he said. 'But there is no gift that you can give them that is greater than the gift of freedom.'

'Do you do this to other animals too?' asked Madlyn. 'Rescue them and heal them, and let them go?'

Dr Manners nodded. 'I have a mission,' he said. 'It came to me when I was a little boy and saying my prayers by my mother's side. I had to work hard to get the money – you won't believe how hard I worked. I was a surgeon in London and often I did six or seven operations in a single day, trying to help spoilt women who were never satisfied. But as soon as I had saved enough, I came here. I won't speak of the things I've seen – we have chickens here that were on their way to be turned into nuggets because they have fowl pest. But fowl pest can be cured, if you spend the time and the money – and we are curing them. I could tell you many such stories but I won't distress you. But you must understand we work outside the law.'

'Like Robin Hood,' said Rollo.

'Yes, like that. But remember that outlaws work in secret. If you breathe a word about what you have seen here on the island, your cattle will be slaughtered and buried even now. You understand that?' The children nodded and Dr Manners pressed a button on his desk.

'Show my visitors out,' he said to the secretary who came. 'Drive them over the causeway – they've had enough walking for one day.'

Left alone, Manners leaned back in his chair and smiled. Then he pressed the buzzer again and his second in command, Dr Fangster, came into the room. He was a small man, as dark as Manners was fair – and formidably clever.

'Any news from the boat?' asked Manners.

Fangster nodded. 'We've had a signal. They're hoping to get here tonight.'

'Good. Good.'

It looked as though the biggest mission they had yet attempted was on course.

Twenty-one

Sir George had not been in London for some time and he didn't realize how much it had changed. He used to stay at his club, which was very quiet and full of other old people reading the paper who said 'shush' if anyone talked – but it had all been modernized with piped music in the rooms and instead of waiters whom you could ask for the things you wanted, there were vending machines with instructions which Sir George couldn't read because the print was too small.

And when he arrived at the Ministry of Animal Health, his troubles really began. He went into the outer office and told one of the secretaries that he wanted to see someone about Klappert's Disease and the secretary said that before he could even ask to see anyone he had to have proof of identity, preferably a passport or driving licence.

So Sir George went back to his club and fetched his driving licence and went back to the ministry and then another secretary told him he had to go to the police station and get a certificate to say he hadn't been involved in any criminal offence. And when he had done that they told him he would have to get his fingerprints taken and have a blood test. And so it went on. By the end of the first afternoon Sir George had got as far as being allowed into the waiting room where one could see the secretary who made the actual appointments with the minister, and she told him that the minister was in a meeting and Sir George should come back tomorrow and try again.

Up to now Sir George had kept his temper, but now he went purple in the face and raised his stick and there would have been one secretary the less at the ministry, but just at that moment a porter came in and said there was an urgent message for Sir George at his club and would he telephone his sister immediately.

And when Sir George picked up the telephone he forgot all about the idiots at the ministry and about Klappert's Disease and his cattle, because what Emily had to tell him was that the children had disappeared. At about the time that Sir George was packing to go back to Clawstone, the eldest of the banshees woke up from her afternoon nap in a very excited state.

'I've had such an exciting dream,' she said, clutching her sister. 'In fact, it was so exciting I'm not sure that it was a dream. It may have been a vision.'

The middle banshee, who had been dozing on the other sofa, sat bolt upright. 'But that's extraordinary. I've had an amazing dream too. It was so vivid I thought it must be telling me something important.'

And now the youngest sister, who preferred to take her afternoon nap in an armchair, said, 'You may or may not believe it, but I too have had a most powerful and important dream.'

The eldest banshee sat up. 'Was it . . . by any chance . . . a dream . . .' she hesitated, 'a dream about a funeral?'

'Yes, it was! It was!' cried the other two. 'That's exactly what it was! It was a dream about a funeral!'

'And was it in the north . . . very far north, this funeral?'

'It was indeed,' said the middle banshee. 'It was further north than you can get and still stay in England.'

The youngest banshee nodded. 'In fact it wasn't in England at all,' she said. 'When I think about it carefully, I see that it was in Scotland. In a small church by the sea.'

'Such a bleak place,' said the eldest banshee.

'So windy.'

'But beautiful. Unspoilt. Remote.'

'Yes.'

For a few minutes the three sisters sat in silence, awed and humbled by their amazing experience. Of course, sisters who live together do often catch each other's thoughts and even each other's dreams, but this seemed to be more than that. It was as though they were being given a message from above.

It was not till they were drinking their second cup of tea from the blue teapot that the eldest banshee dared to ask another question.

'Did this funeral . . . did it go well?'

Her sisters put down their cups.

'Oh, no,' said the middle sister.

'No, no,' said the youngest one. 'It didn't go well at all. It was a disaster. An absolutely shocking mess. No wonder they were so upset. The undertaker should have been sacked.'

'All in all, it's a wonder how the poor things managed to go on with their lives at all.'

'Though of course it wasn't exactly their *lives* they went on with.'

There was a long pause. A very long pause indeed. Because by the time they got to their third cup of tea and the mists of sleep had left them, the banshees were realizing that their dream had not come to them out of the blue. It was only partly a dream. It was a dream about something they had once experienced. It was a buried memory which had come up while they slept. When they were young they had been to just such a funeral and seen the disaster that had happened there.

'I knew we'd seen the poor things before,' said the eldest banshee.

'Me too. As soon as we met them at the gravel pit, I felt as though I knew them.'

All three sisters nodded their heads.

'But the question is,' said the oldest banshee, 'what do we do now? Do we leave well alone? Or do we see what we can do?'

Her sisters sighed. 'We'd better see how we feel in the morning,' they said.

But they knew really. When a great wrong has been done to someone, it has to be put right. There isn't really any doubt about that.

Twenty-two

The last thing the children had wanted was to spend another night in the chapel.

'We must get back *quickly*,' said Madlyn. 'They'll be so worried about us.'

But how?

They had come up to Blackscar in the warden's car in a panic and in the night. Now they couldn't believe they'd had the nerve to do it.

'I'm worried about the clutch,' said Mr Smith. 'I don't want to do any more damage.'

But the matter was settled for them, because when they tried to start the engine nothing happened.

'The battery's flat,' said Ned gloomily. 'We'll have to walk to the next village and get a bus, and then a train.'

Madlyn had taken some money from the Open Day tin before they left; there would probably be enough to take them some of the way at least, and when they were clear of the island they could phone Sir George.

There was a timetable tacked to the noticeboard in the church porch, and a map. There was one bus a day from a village called Seaforth three miles away, but they had missed it.

The ghosts were not sorry to have another night to rest. They had felt unwell and uncomfortable in the hotel. Perhaps it was the central heating, or Dr

Manners's toilet water, but Brenda said she had a headache and Ranulf 's rat was off his food. Not that Ranulf wanted to have his heart chewed exactly, but when you are used to something you are used to it.

But the real nuisance was The Feet. They had had to pick up The Feet by force and carry them to the island, and as soon as they got back they had run off to the tombstone labelled ISH again and dug their toes into the moss and refused to move.

They would have been angry at such bad behaviour except that The Feet were so worried and distressed. Every time they were told to come away from the tombstone, drops of sweat broke out all over their skin.

'If it *is* sweat,' said Rollo. 'Perhaps it's tears.'

The thought that The Feet were crying was of course very upsetting. 'But we can't just leave them here,' said Sunita.

So all in all the ghosts were very glad to rest for another night.

And while they slept a boat chugged quietly into Blackscar bay and tied up at the jetty.

It was a forty-foot trawler, scruffy and battered, with knotted pine planking. It could have been any fishing boat, but fixed to the forward deck was a large harpoon gun.

The boat was a whaler and it was flying the Norwegian flag.

No one was up yet; it would be dark for at least another two hours. The sailors – rough-looking men – turned in to their bunks. Presently they would unload the cargo they had brought, but now they slept.

The Feet felt the slight vibration of the trawler's

engine as they lay under the tombstone, but they did not move. But Rollo heard the noise of the engine and woke . . . and crept out of the church and climbed up the grassy hill that gave a view over the whole island. The boat had come in, just as Dr Manners had said, to take the cattle to the promised land. He watched for a while; then, as the light grew stronger, he took out Uncle George's binoculars.

It was a very small boat to transport a whole herd of cattle. It was really very small.

And something nagged at the back of his mind. Something about one of the men he had seen out of the window in Dr Manners's room – a man he thought he had seen before . . .

The Mundanians were in their wooden hut, eating their breakfast of beans and fermented goat curd.

There were eight of them: a very old woman with a single gold tooth, a younger, buxom one, and six men, all living in a space the size of a caravan. The huts on either side of them housed chickens.

They looked tired, and the day that faced them would be as hard as all the others. Cleaning out the animal houses, incinerating the waste matter, humping heavy loads to and from the workshops . . . and other things that they tried not to think about.

Today there was an extra job – unloading the cargo which the whaler had brought.

The hut was bare and cold; the Mundanians could not afford proper heating and their food was what they could scrape from the soil. They were so poor that they could buy nothing, and in any case they were forbidden to go to the mainland.

144

Dr Manners had not been lying when he said that the Mundanians came from a very beautiful country high in the mountains of central Europe, and that they were of proud and ancient stock. But the Mundanians had not come to Blackscar because they had heard of Manners's missionary work; they had never even heard of Blackscar. What had happened was that two years earlier a cruel dictator from a neighbouring country had conquered Mundania and started a reign of terror. He had forbidden the Mundanians to speak their language or have their own schools or practise their own religion, and when anyone protested they were imprisoned or killed.

So the two brothers, Slavek and Izaak had taken their family – their old mother, Slavek's wife and four male cousins – and trekked across Europe to look for a place where they could live in peace. And after months of hardship they had reached Great Britain, thinking they would find a welcome there and a home and a chance to work.

They were horribly wrong. The whole family was shut up in a squalid and overcrowded camp surrounded by barbed wire and told they had no right to work and no permits and no papers and would be sent back to Mundania.

Twice they had been shifted to other camps that were even more crowded and wretched than the first. Then the third time they were moved they managed to escape, and it was as they were trudging the roads that a man had come and offered them work at Blackscar. Not paid work of course (they were not allowed to be paid) and work that was harder than any that was ever done even by the humblest peasant

145

in Mundania, but they knew that if they complained they would be sent back to the camp. They were really prisoners at Blackscar and each day they woke up so wretched and sad and homesick that they did not know how they would bear it. But they did bear it. They had no choice.

So now they finished their goat curd and while Slavek and Izaak went out to fetch the cargo from the whaling ship, the old woman with the gold tooth piled up the dirty dishes.

But before she started on the washing up, she turned on the ancient transistor radio which one of the workmen had given them.

On the whaler they had started unloading. There were four long canvas bags – not a big load but valuable, incredibly valuable; the sailors expected to be paid an enormous amount of money, and they had earned it. The risks they had taken to get their booty had been great; if they had been caught they wouldn't just have been fined, they could have been imprisoned.

Although the boat flew the Norwegian flag, the men were not Norwegians. They were crooks and riffraff from several countries, but they had one thing in common: they were hunters who knew the sea and cared nothing for the creatures that lived in it if they could make a profit by killing them. To get the booty they were now unloading, they had harpooned close on thirty whales – and not those whales that it was legal to hunt, but rare and protected ones.

The whales they had killed were narwhals, those shy and gentle beasts which live in the icy waters of the Arctic and are rarely seen by man.

Narwhals are not large as whales go, they are seldom more than five metres long. The Vikings called them 'corpse whales', not because they ate corpses – they wouldn't dream of doing such a thing – but because of the blue-grey colour of their skins.

But though they are small, there is one thing about male narwhals that is extraordinary. Growing out of their foreheads is an enormous, single, spiral horn.

Because they are so rare and so amazing, narwhal horns have been prized throughout history. Medieval princes believed they could detect poison which had been put in someone's food by an enemy. In Asian countries, doctors ground them up for potions and medicines. Carved narwhal horns adorned the palaces of kings.

And just as poachers will hunt elephants for their tusks and leave them to rot once the ivory has been removed, so the sailors who had come now to Blackscar had cut the horns from the narwhals they had slaughtered and thrown the carcasses back into the sea.

Dr Manners too prized narwhal horns – but not to detect poison or to use for potions. He wanted them for quite a different reason. It was a reason that nobody but him and his assistant, Dr Fangster, knew anything about.

Slavek and Izaak had begun to wheel the canvas bags up to the office beside the main laboratory. The bags were padlocked; no one was allowed to open them; what was in them was a strict secret, but the Mundanians were used to shifting loads they knew nothing about. When they were safely stored, and

Dr Manners had examined the contents, he would arrange for the sailors to be paid.

They stowed the bags and went back to the hut to fetch their tools for the day's work.

'Good heavens – what is it, what is the matter?' asked Izaak as he threw open the door.

The old woman was sobbing in one corner; Slavek's wife moaned in the other. The four cousins, who should already have been mucking out the animal houses, were huddled over the radio. Their faces too were streaked with tears.

'What is it?' repeated Izaak. 'For goodness' sake, what's wrong?'

The cousins turned from the radio, and wiped their eyes.

'It has happened,' they cried, throwing their arms round the brothers. 'Oh, Slavek, Izaak – it has happened at last! That we should live to see this day!'

On the hill opposite the island, Rollo watched the boat. The sailors had finished unloading; soon now the cattle would go on board. Dr Manners had said they would be washed clean first, restored to their whiteness. Only how would they all fit in? Dr Manners knew everything there was to know about animals; he would not let them travel in cramped or unsuitable conditions; but all the same, the boat was small.

And what about the man who had walked past the windows of the hotel? Of course, he might have been somebody quite different, but if not . . .

From the doorway of the church, Madlyn called up to him.

148

'Come on, Rollo. It's time to go.'

They had packed up; anything they could not carry was locked in the car. It was going to be a long trek to the village.

But if Rollo heard her, he took no notice. When she looked again, she saw that he had left the hill and was running down the beach towards the causeway.

'Come back,' she yelled. 'Come back at once.'

But Rollo went on running.

'We can't let him go alone,' said Ned.

'One day I'm going to kill him,' said Madlyn, as they set off in pursuit. 'What's more, I shall enjoy doing it. I shall enjoy killing him.'

They caught up with him as he crouched behind a boulder overlooking the bay and the jetty, and dropped down beside him. The boat was still tied up, there were no signs of any preparations for loading the cattle.

'What on earth are you up to?' said Madlyn angrily.

But before Rollo could explain, they heard a hissing noise – a noise like 'Psst' but not really an English 'Psst'. Then a swarthy face with a curving black moustache appeared round the side of the boulder, followed by a second face like the first.

It was the two men who had caught them and taken them to Dr Manners, but they looked different. Not fierce now but almost smiling – and they carried no pitchforks or wooden sticks.

'You come with us,' said the first man. 'We show you something. Quick! We not hurt you.'

'We not hurt you,' repeated the second man. 'Please, you come. Now.'

The children came.

They were led into a low wooden hut. They had seen it when they were looking for the cattle, but it hadn't seemed like the sort of place that people lived in; it looked more like a shed for animals, a chicken house or a pigsty.

But people certainly lived in it. They not only lived in it, they were having a party. There were candles on the table and a wooden platter piled with pancakes. Red and green and purple paper streamers were tacked to the walls. In one corner a man was playing a mouth harp, making music that was both reedy and exciting, and the men were dancing, their arms resting on each other's shoulders, while the women twirled round and round, sending their heavy skirts spinning. From the crackly radio came the sound of an excited voice talking in a language the children had never heard. Then the voice stopped and a blaring military tune was played, and when it came on everybody stopped dancing and stood to attention and the women beat their chests.

The children were completely bewildered. Why had they been brought here? Were they going to be frogmarched away, or beaten, or tied up as part of this strange feast? But instead they were handed glasses of a colourless fiery liquid and told to drink a toast.

'Mundania – the Motherland!' cried their hosts, and tossed their glasses over their shoulders, and the children did the same.

But at last there was a lull, the radio was turned down and packing cases were pulled out for the children to sit on while the Mundanians explained what had happened.

'Is revolution in our country,' said Slavek – and to

make it clear he stuck out two fingers and said, 'Bang, bang!'

'Bad man has gone – dead,' put in Izaak happily.

With all the Mundanians helping out with words and gestures, the children gathered that the dictator who had terrorized their country had been overthrown. It was news of the revolution that they had heard on the radio, and now they were free to go home.

'Home,' they repeated joyfully, nodding their heads and smiling. 'We go home.'

But the children had not been called in just to hear the good news. There was something which the Mundanians wanted them to do and it was important.

'We call you because you must see what is here happening. You must tell and you must make stop.'

'Yes, yes,' said the other Mundanians. 'You must go quick from island and make it to stop.'

'But what is it?' asked Madlyn. 'What is it we must stop?'

Slavek's face was grim.

'We show. Now. But you must very quiet be. You must cripp.'

'Cripp?'

'Cripp like mouses. And stay behind from me.'

He turned and took a bunch of keys from a shelf. Then he led the children from the hut across a covered way and unlocked a door.

'Zis,' he said. 'Zis you must stop.'

The children never forgot the sight that met their eyes. They were in an experimental chicken house but the birds, each in a separate cage, were not really like chickens. They were much larger, and a flap of skin had formed across their claws so that they had become web-footed. But the horrifying thing was their beaks. Their beaks had been stretched and on some of the birds a strange, shovel-like protrusion had been grafted on.

'But what is it? Why are they like that?' asked Madlyn.

Rollo was shivering.

'I know why. I know what the experiment is for. They're trying to turn the chickens into dodos.'

Slavek nodded. 'Yes. Yes. Dr Manners he makes dodos because they are not any more.'

'They're extinct,' put in Ned.

But the dodos were only the beginning. Slavek's key now unlocked a steamy room in which a small alligator lay on the edge of a shallow pond. He was absolutely still and pressing down on his snout was a heavy weight. A clamp fixed it and it was connected to a pressure gauge.

Even Rollo did not know what was happening here.

'They make heavier and then more heavy, so snout is flat. Make new animal.'

The creature lay still, unable to move; its yellow eyes were dull. It was completely helpless.

Rollo had connected now. 'I know. A gavial. They're becoming extinct. They have these long flattened snouts. Oh God, the poor beast can't move.'

But that was not nearly the end.

They passed through two double doors into an aviary. The grey parrots who sat there were chained tightly to their perches. Their eyes were shut. One had fallen over sideways and could not right itself. And all

152

the time, relentlessly, they were being squirted with jets of dye from a computerized spray: jets of crimson, of violet, of blue . . .

'Here he makes – how do you call it? – Imperial Parrot. Not any more in jungle, all gone. So people want and they come and buy. Buy for much, much money.' Slavek shook his head. 'Many die, but they get more.'

Now came the worst of all. A gorilla, lying slumped in the corner of his cage. One foot was bandaged, his eyes were glazed, his breath came in shallow gasps.

'He's going to die,' said Rollo.

'Yes. They try to take foot and move it so toes go other way. They try to make – how do you say? Abominable Man.'

'An Abominable Snowman,' said Ned. 'A yeti. Their feet are supposed to be back to front.'

Slavek locked the door of the room and turned to the children.

'There is more,' he said. 'It is for money, money, money . . .' He made a gesture rubbing his fingers together. 'People come – they want what is not. They pay and they pay and they pay and Dr Manners he grow very rich.'

'A centre for making extinct animals,' said Ned. 'It's incredible.'

But they could believe it. People paid fortunes for rare and unusual animals. How much more would they pay for animals which were extinct – or mythical?

Back in the hut they saw that the Mundanians' few possessions had been packed away. There were only three bags on the floor, which seemed to contain their worldly goods. The women wore their shawls, the

153

men had buttoned up their jackets.

'You must go quick and tell police,' they said again. 'We could not – we haf no money, no papers, we were as slaves, and now we go home. But you will tell.'

'But how will you get home without money?' asked Madlyn. 'What will you do?'

The men smiled. 'We haf plan,' said Slavek, tapping the side of his nose, and the others nodded and said, 'Yes, we haf plan.'

It was only now that Rollo was recovered enough to ask the question that burned him up.

'But what about the cattle?' said Rollo. 'What will happen to them? Why have they brought the cattle here?'

Remembering what he had seen, he began to shiver again.

The Mundanians exchanged glances.

'We do not know,' said Slavek, 'but it is big what will happen to the cows. It is very big, very important. It is big and it is soon. He waits for the boat to bring him what he needs, and now the boat has come.'

His brother nodded. 'It is big with the cows,' he said. 'I think perhaps it is tonight.'

Then they shook hands one by one. 'You can rest here,' they said. 'But soon you must go back and tell.'

And the children were left alone.

Twenty-three

The Mundanians had gone. The three children huddled together in the empty hut, stunned by what they had seen. They had to get back to the mainland and tell the world about this evil place – and quickly.

Ned opened the door a crack.

'There's no one about. If we drop down on to the beach and go round by the shore we should make it.' They hadn't gone far when they heard a sound which brought them up short: the desolate yet frantic mooing of a cow who has been separated from her calf. Then men shouting orders, the stamping of hooves . . .

'It is big what will happen with the cows,' the brothers had said. 'It is big and it is soon. Perhaps it is tonight.'

Without hesitation, the children turned and ran back towards the buildings.

They had come to a kind of forecourt, a concreted yard with drainage channels which had been swabbed down with disinfectant. A big incinerator took up one side of the courtyard. On the other side was a very large building: grey and forbidding and windowless. It looked like an aircraft hangar or an industrial workshop.

Beside the incinerator was a row of large waste bins. The children ducked down behind them and waited.

They waited for what seemed a very long time. And then slowly – very slowly – the huge steel double doors began to draw apart. The gap grew wide, and wider – and there, as on a stage, lit up by arc lamps more brilliant and dazzling than any daylight, they saw an operating table, high and clinical and white. Chrome cylinders of oxygen stood beside it, and pressure gauges and trolleys loaded with jars of liquid and coils of rubber tubing. And close by was a rack of glittering, outsize instruments: scalpels and scissors and forceps and clamps.

Rollo gasped and Madlyn put an arm round his shoulder.

There was no one in the lab at first, but then a man in a white coat came in from a door at the back and walked over to a large sink and pulled out a long curled horn that had been soaking there.

The man turned, and they saw his face.

It was the vet with the black beard who had come to Clawstone to tell them that the cattle were sick. He had shaved off his beard but they knew him at once. It was this man that Rollo had glimpsed out of the window of the hotel.

But before they could work out what this meant they heard the sound of hooves and, walking past them, his head hanging, came a calf, led by a man in overalls.

The calf was snow-white and it walked as slowly as the beasts must have walked in the olden days on the way to the temple to be sacrificed, sensing their terrible fate. When it reached the stream of light coming from the double doors, it stiffened its legs and tried to dig its hooves into the concrete, but they

156

slipped on the wet floor and the man jerked the rope and led it forward.

Rollo had recognized it at once. It was the youngest calf, the one he had watched being born. His calf.

Ned held him back as he tried to leap out of his hiding place.

'Wait,' he hissed. 'We have to know.'

The man leading the calf tugged at the rope once more and the calf was dragged into the operating theatre.

The door on the right opened again and Dr Manners came in. He was dressed in a high-necked operating gown; a surgical mask was strung round his neck.

'Is everything ready, Fangster?' he asked, and the vet who had called himself Dr Dale nodded and lifted up the curled horn with the pointed end which he had taken from the bag that the whalers had brought ashore.

'This is the smallest. We'll need to pack the wound tight, but it should close over all right. And if not . . .' He shrugged.

'Quite so,' said Dr Manners.

The calf was dragged up on to the operating table. It was mad with fear, fighting every inch of the way.

Dr Manners was filling a great syringe. The vet picked up the narwhal horn and held it above the head of the tethered beast.

And in that instant the children understood everything.

Twenty-four

It had begun in a faraway country, in the Kingdom of Barama, with a small, unhealthy prince who could not sleep.

Barama is in South America and it is very beautiful. It lies between Venezuela to the east and Guyana to the west and many people have not even heard of it, although the man who rules it is possibly the richest person in the world.

Barama is very beautiful; it has a palm-fringed coastline and mountains covered in green-blue trees and meadows filled with flowers. But what makes Barama special is one thing and one thing only: oil.

Oil gushes and bursts and erupts out of the sandy desert, and the more it is dug up and barrelled and sold to oil-hungry countries, the more seems to come out of the ground.

Before the oil was found, the princes of Barama led busy and active lives. They were strong men with big moustaches and they hunted and shot and fought their neighbours and each other.

But as they became richer and richer all this changed. They built themselves enormous palaces and filled them with priceless furniture. They bought themselves cars and aeroplanes and yachts and they covered their wives and daughters with fabulous jewels. They bought hundreds of suits and pairs of shoes and sumptuous ceremonial robes, and ate larger and larger meals and got more and more servants to wait on them.

The result of all this was exactly what you would expect. They became bored and miserable. Their muscles got flabby because they never walked anywhere but were always driven in cars and their stomachs boiled and bubbled with indigestion from all the rich food that they ate. So while their palaces got bigger and bigger, the rulers of Barama got smaller and sadder and feebler, and the present ruler of Barama, King Carlos, was a very little man indeed.

Carlos had not been a healthy child. His muscles were so weak that a servant used to go upstairs behind him and help to push his leg up to the next tread, and he had mostly been fed on slops – semolina pudding and lentil soups and things of that sort, because solid food gave him a stomach ache.

Prince Carlos's mother had died when he was a baby, and after that his father had married five more times, choosing women from all over the world. Having five stepmothers had made little Carlos very worried and unhappy – there wasn't one among them who had loved him or been kind – and when Carlos's father had divorced them they had gone off in a huff, with their jewels and their money, and the little boy had never seen them again.

But there was one person in the child's life who never went away, and that was his nurse, Nadia.

Nadia had come to Barama from a long way away – from the border of Russia and China. By the time she came to Barama the little prince was so unhealthy and spoilt and sad that he couldn't get to sleep at night and lay in his canopied bed in his vast bedroom, staring at the ceiling and imagining devils and ghouls armed to the teeth who would fly down and cut his throat.

Nadia was sorry for the frightened little boy whom nobody loved, and she sat by his bed, night after night, and told him stories.

The stories Nadia told were the ones she had been told in her own faraway country. They were stories about mythical beasts – good kind beasts who helped travellers and comforted wayfarers. She told him about griffins and dragons and horses with wings. She told him about dogs that could speak and golden cockerels and kindly snakes that wound themselves round children and kept them from harm – and she told him about one beast in particular, a beast which her people loved more than any other in the world. And when she sat beside little Carlos and spoke in her soft, low voice, he could sleep.

Then came the day when Carlos's father was drowned, diving off his latest yacht, and Carlos became the ruler of Barama.

He could now do anything he liked, but the trouble was he didn't know what he did like. His five stepmothers had put him off women and his indigestion put him off food and there wasn't really any work to do governing his country because his ministers did it perfectly well.

For a while he drifted sadly through his palaces, and sat gloomily in his Turkish baths and bought a large number of dressing gowns with gold tassels which he stumbled over.

But one day as he was staring miserably out of the window, he had a vision. He would make a great

160

garden – a paradise garden – and he would fill it with rare trees and with beautiful flowers and animals that you could see nowhere else: with the animals that Nadia had told him about in her stories. And above all with the beast she had said was the most beautiful and gentle and powerful of all – the beast which her people had loved more than any other in the world.

If he could get this amazing, swift and gentle creature for his paradise garden he thought he would be a happy man. So he called together his advisors and his courtiers and his ministers and told them what he wanted.

'Only I don't just want one,' he said. 'The Kings of Barama never have one of anything. I want a whole herd.'

So his advisors began to look for somebody who could get the King what he wanted, and after a long search they found Dr Maurice Manners of the Blackscar Animal Centre in Great Britain.

When Dr Manners heard what the King of Barama wanted, he hesitated. It was the biggest order he had ever had and there were all sorts of technical difficulties – but when he learnt that the King was offering five million pounds, he stopped hesitating quite quickly and tried to think what could be done.

Manners had come to Blackscar after a series of unfortunate accidents to the ladies he had operated on so as to make them more beautiful. There was a tummy tuck which had gone septic and a nose job which had ended up behind the patient's ears, and, instead of standing by him and protecting him, his fellow doctors had said he was a disgrace to the profession and he was not allowed to be a doctor any more.

Some people would have been so hurt that they would have given up, but not Dr Manners. He had met up with a brilliant vet called Dr Fangster, who was bored with simply making animals better and had worked out all sorts of interesting experiments, like joining one animal's lungs to another animal's heart and then to a third animal's stomach, and together they had come up with the idea for the Blackscar Centre.

For, as Manners said, if people want animals that don't exist and will pay a lot of money for them, we will simply *make* these creatures. Between us we know everything there is to know about implants and bone grafts and tissue transfers, so what's to stop us turning a chicken into a dodo or an ostrich into an auk? What's more, the people we supply will be so pleased to get their animal they'll be certain they're getting the real thing.

And Manners was right. The collectors believed what they wanted to believe and hid the rare beasts they had asked for in secret zoos and private parks all over the world.

Nevertheless, when the order came through from the King of Barama, they had at first been baffled. It would mean getting hold of a herd of pure white horses and that would take a long time and be very expensive. But when they started to look up what was written about the beasts they were supposed to be making they learned something very interesting. Their hooves had not been rounded and solid like the hooves of horses; they had been split in the centre.

162

The beasts had been cloven-footed. Their feet had a cleft in them like the feet of cows or sheep or goats.

Not only that, but all the books which Manners and the vet consulted were agreed on one thing: the creatures came of absolutely pure bloodstock, and always bred true.

And when they heard about the Wild White Cattle of Clawstone Park, they knew that their search was over – and that the King of Barama would get his unicorns.

Twenty-five

Dr Manners stepped up to the operating table. He pulled on his rubber gloves. He smiled. The calf lay helpless and tethered, silent now, its eyes rolling in terror.

'Time to anaesthetize the patient,' he said.

This was the beginning: the first calf in the world to be turned into a unicorn. They had chosen a young one because the tissues were soft – it would be easier to make a hole in its forehead and implant the narwhal horn – and because its own horns were not yet formed, it would not be necessary to scoop them out, as they would have to do with the larger animals. Of course, being so young, it was more likely to die during the operation, but there were plenty more of the beasts in the paddock.

Five million pounds' worth of beasts . . .

The sawn-off narwhal horn was ready in its jar of disinfectant. It was incredible how like a unicorn's horn it was: no wonder narwhals in the olden days had been called the unicorn fish. An assistant, also gowned and masked, had laid out the sterile instruments: the razor to shave a patch between the creature's ears; the drill to bore a hole in its skull, the scalpels and sutures and pads of cotton wool. A cylinder of blood for emergencies stood on a trolley close by.

'See to the doors,' ordered Manners.

The assistant pressed a button and the doors to the forecourt moved together.

Outside, the children threw themselves frantically against the heavy steel partitions, trying to push them apart.

It was impossible. There was only a small gap now and it was shrinking fast. Rollo managed to slip through, and then Madlyn.

But not Ned. Before he could follow, the doors clanged relentlessly shut and Ned was left outside.

Dr Manners had reached for the syringe. It was poised above the head of the little calf; he was about to plunge the needle into a vein on its throat.

It was at this moment that Madlyn and Rollo almost fell into the room.

'Well well, what have we here?' the doctor said. And then in his usual calm voice: 'Tie them up. We'll deal with them later.' He turned to the children. 'Since you're here you might as well watch. It isn't every nosy child who sees the creation of a completely new beast.'

'You can't,' shouted Rollo. 'You—'

And then a hand came down over his mouth.

The children had no chance against Fangster and the assistant as they were thrown to the floor and trussed up with surgical tape. They were as defenceless as the wretched beast on the operating table.

And there was nobody to help them. They were quite alone.

The operation was going forward now. Fangster had selected his razor, the assistant had taken the drill out of its sterile wrapping.

Manners had put the syringe down on the trolley to deal with the children. Now he put out his hand to reach for it.

Except that it wasn't there. It had rolled over twice on a perfectly flat surface and crashed on to the floor.

'What on earth are you doing, you idiot?' shouted Manners.

'It wasn't me,' said Fangster angrily. 'I didn't touch it.' He turned to the assistant. 'You must have knocked it with your arm.'

'No, I didn't. I wasn't anywhere near.'

'Prepare another one,' ordered Manners.

A second syringe was taken from its wrapping and filled with anaesthetic. Manners was angry now. He jabbed the point of the needle hard into the throat of the little calf, which gave a bellow of pain.

But before he could press in the plunger, the syringe jerked itself out of his hand, flew up into the air, and impaled itself in a fire bucket.

Manners took a deep breath. There wasn't really anything wrong. It was just operation nerves. People didn't realize that even the most famous surgeons felt anxious before an important operation. He was seeing things.

Fangster had pulled the narwhal horn out of its jar and was holding it. And then suddenly he wasn't holding it any more. The horn was floating quite by itself up into the air . . . high it floated and higher, before it did a somersault and came down again behind him.

'Ow, ow – what are you doing?' yelled Fangster at the assistant. 'Stop it, that hurts!'

'I'm not doing anything,' said the assistant. 'It's the

horn – it's digging itself into your backside.'

Madlyn managed to turn her head and look at Rollo. They had felt alone and friendless and they had been wrong.

Manners had pulled himself together. If he couldn't make the syringe work, he'd have to stun the creature instead.

'Get me a hammer,' he shouted. But before the assistant could obey him, a coil of rubber tubing had unwound itself slowly . . . very slowly, like a snake uncoiling from a long sleep, and then – still slowly – it rose, floated dreamily across to Manners and began to wind itself around the doctor's neck.

'Ugh! Glup! Let go,' spluttered the doctor.

'Brenda,' whispered Madlyn. 'She does so love strangling.'

Fangster was going wild. He went to pull a scalpel out of the rack, determined to make an incision and implant the horn somehow – but before he could reach for the scalpel, the scalpel reached for him. It moved by itself out of the rack and came towards him, and he just had time to duck as it flew past him and embedded itself in the wall.

An arc lamp on the ceiling swayed, then crashed to the ground. Sunita always did her best work on ceilings. A second lamp followed it – and a splinter of glass hit the assistant on the shoulder.

'I'm off,' he cried, and disappeared through the door at the back.

A cylinder of blood fell on its side. The sticky liquid oozed out on to the floor and Fangster slipped and lay on his back.

'Stop it,' he screamed to the empty air. 'Get off me.

167

I know you're there, I can feel you. Stop tramping on my chest.'

The children turned to each other. So The Feet too had put aside their own troubles and come to help.

Manners had managed to tear himself free from the rubber tubing. But now he went berserk. He seized the drill with its lethally sharp point and rushed at the children. It was their fault. This madness had started when they got in. Crunching through broken glass, slithering, cursing, Manners lifted his arm, ready to bring the point down on Rollo's head.

What happened next was so ghastly that Manners thought he would die of it. His head was thrust back by an invisible hand. He was seized and shaken, and beaten and punched . . . but that was not the worst of it. As he fell back against the wall there was a kind of flurry as though something was being dislodged.

And then he felt claws scrabbling across his face. He could not see them but he knew that they were there – grey and vile and utterly obscene. And after the claws, trailing across his cheek, came something long and cold and scaly. A tail . . .

Then, from the dark nothingness that was attacking him, there came a scream.

Ned had wasted no time after the doors clanged shut and left him outside.

Somehow he had to get a message through to Sir George and the police – but how? And then he remembered the whaler tied up to the jetty. All seagoing ships had a short-wave radio. If only he wasn't too late.

The boat was still there – but there were signs of

168

activity; ropes being coiled, the sound of an engine starting, and men moving purposefully on the deck. It was only now that he was afraid that they wouldn't let him use the radio. Men who poached the rarest and loveliest of whales would not be the kind that helped people in need.

Then, as he ran along the jetty, he noticed something strange. The Norwegian flag had gone and a new flag had been hoisted in its place.

It was a most unusual flag, made up of a pair of long red underpants, a green scarf and a purple cap.

Where had he seen those colours before? Of course! On the walls of the Mundanians' hut. They were the national colours of Mundania! And now the man who had been coiling the rope turned.

'So! What you do here?' said Slavek. 'You must go to tell—'

Ned in a rush of words explained. 'I need to use the radio. I need someone to send a message, please, *please*. They're in such danger!'

Slavek nodded. 'Come with me.'

He led him into a cubicle where a man in oilskins was sitting, guarded by one of Slavek's cousins with a gun.

'We have taken over boat,' said Slavek cheerfully. 'Now we go home.' He prodded the radio operator. 'When he has sent your message we throw him in sea with the others.'

'Really?'

'Of course. We need boat.'

'But what will happen to them?'

Slavek shrugged.

'They can swim, perhaps. Is pity, because they are bad men.'

The last thing Ned saw as he raced back to the lab was the old lady with the gold tooth leaning over the railings, waving goodbye.

The steel doors were open. The lab was a welter of broken glass, spilt liquid and upturned furniture. Rollo was hanging on to the rope of the calf. Madlyn was bent over a sink, trying not to be sick.

And the ghosts had become visible – but although they had saved the children and the calf, they did not look triumphant or victorious.

They were clustered anxiously round Ranulf, who was sitting on a locker with his head in his hands. No wonder that this stately and dignified ghost had given such a dreadful scream. Ranulf 's shirt was open, and something – obviously – was most seriously wrong.

Of Manners and Fangster there was no sign.

They had locked themselves into the cloakroom. It was the room where they scrubbed up before operations: white and clinical and disinfected. There were a row of basins, a shower and two toilets in adjacent cubicles.

They were safe here. The door of the cloakroom was barred, and if necessary they could retreat further, into the toilets, and lock them too.

'They won't . . . get us . . . here,' said Manners. His teeth were chattering and he had bruises on his cheek from one of the canisters which had flown through the air and hit him. The vet was the colour of cheese and was trembling uncontrollably. Both men had forgotten unicorns and the millions of pounds they had hoped to make. All they wanted now was to save their skins.

And then they saw that something had happened to the door. It was still tightly shut, but in the wooden panel there had appeared a kind of fuzziness . . . a shimmering shape which leaped down on to the floor and crept towards them.

'It's a rat,' screeched Manners, backing away.

But not an ordinary rat. A rat out of the vilest of dreams: huge and misshapen and scabrous, with yellow teeth and with a body that wavered and flickered and disappeared and then re-formed itself.

Slowly, it crawled forward, opening its mouth, searching – and then stopped.

'Shoo! Shoo – go away.'

Fangster grabbed the toilet brush and hit the animal hard across the back. There was a strange, squelchy sound and the rat vanished.

'It's gone!'

'No. No. Look, it's re-formed itself. Oh Lord, it's obscene!'

The rat moved closer and the two men backed away, gibbering with fear. This was the worst thing so far, this disgusting, shape-changing thing, looking for something to chew.

'Maybe we could jump over it and make a dash for it,' suggested Manners.

But as soon as they moved, the rat moved too – sitting up on its hind legs, chomping . . . seeking . . .

It had come very close to Manners's foot; it opened its mouth.

But what it found was wrong. It did not want hard

non-ectoplasmic shoes; it did not want trouser legs smelling of disinfectant.

The rat wanted what it had always had and needed. It wanted what had violently and suddenly been torn from him. It wanted the familiar hairy chest and well-known heart of the man to whom it belonged.

Shaken and upset and displaced, Ranulf's rat held the two men prisoner and waited.

Twenty-six

Uncle George was a careful driver. His old Bentley usually chugged through the village at not much more than the speed of a tractor.

But he was not driving slowly now. Ever since Ned's message had come over the crackling receiver of a schoolboy in the village who belonged to a radio club, Uncle George had behaved like a maniac.

He had collected his blunderbuss, and his pistol from the war, and his grandfather's fowling piece, ready to blow to smithereens anyone who had harmed the children. Emily wanted to come with him; she had become quite hysterical since she had found that the children had gone.

'I want to be beside you,' she cried. 'I want to shoot somebody too!'

But George had persuaded her that it would be best if she went down to the police station in case they wanted some more particulars. And then, just as he was setting off, a car had drawn up, and out poured three plump ladies in black overcoats who greeted him like long-lost relations, though he had never set eyes on them before.

'Cooee – we're the banshees,' shouted the eldest and plumpest of the ladies. 'We thought we'd call in on our way to Blackscar to tell—'

'Blackscar,' said Uncle George sharply. 'What do

173

you know about Blackscar?'

'Well, it's the most extraordinary thing,' said the eldest banshee. 'We just had a flash!'

'It came to us when we woke from our nap,' said the middle banshee. 'We'd been wondering and wondering ever since we saw them in the gravel pit.'

'So we thought we must go up and make sure, because we could see how troubled they were and when we remembered—'

But Sir George was in no mood to listen to this insane and meaningless babble.

'Could you stand aside, please?' he barked. 'If you want to go to Blackscar you can follow me later.'

But the banshees had taken no notice.

'Don't tell me you're going to Blackscar too? You mean you had the same idea about The Feet and—'

But Sir George had run out of patience.

'Out of my way, ladies,' he snapped.

He opened the door and climbed in, but before he could start the engine the three banshees had got in the back.

'It's amazing. It's such a coincidence! And think how much petrol we'll save! We're all ready, Sir George. Aren't we, girls?'

If there had been one banshee George would have thrown her out. Even two. But throwing three well-fed banshees out of his car was going to take too long. He ground his dentures together and stepped on the accelerator.

So now he drove through the night. The message from the ship giving the location of the island had mentioned the stolen cattle, but to his surprise it was not the cattle he was thinking about, it was the children. He tried to remember how upset he had been when he heard that Rollo and Madlyn were coming for the summer, and now he realized that nothing mattered except that they and Ned were safe.

Sir George was an old man. The drive in the mist and the rain exhausted him more than he would have believed. When at last he came to Blackscar and stopped the car he almost slumped over the wheel.

Then slowly he raised his head. He had stopped at the edge of a small bluff which overlooked the sea and the island.

And what he saw was something out of a story from the beginning of time.

Seemingly walking on the water, came the Wild White Cattle of Clawstone, their horns glinting in the first rays of the morning sun. At their head was the king bull, and sitting on his back, urging him forwards, a shimmering Indian goddess with streaming hair. Behind the king came the old cow with her crumpled horn, limping a little; and then, strung out in single file over the causeway, the rest of his beasts: the angry bull, the two calves who were special friends, the cow who loved stinging nettles . . .

He saw them all and he knew them all. The morning light grew stronger and the shimmering goddess turned into Sunita. And now George saw the children. Water was already lapping over the causeway but they walked steadily, their heads held high. Ned and Madlyn were in front, helping to keep the cattle moving.

And at the end of the procession came Rollo, leading the smallest calf on a rope.

For a moment Sir George just looked, ashamed of the moisture in his eyes. The banshees were asleep. Then he hurried down to the sands. The king bull, finding himself on dry land, bellowed and tossed his head, then set off for a field behind the chapel, and the rest of the cattle followed him.

'Let them be,' said Sir George. 'We'll get them rounded up later.' He could see how dozy the beasts were, still drugged perhaps. They would not roam too far. 'What about you?' he asked the children. 'You're not hurt?'

Ned shook his head. 'We're fine. Madlyn's breathed in some anaesthetic, but she's getting better.' Madlyn nodded. 'I'm all right – but the ghosts are a bit shaky, and Ranulf 's had an awful shock.'

But Sir George was not interested in the ghosts. What he wanted was to get his revenge on the villains.

'Where are they?' he asked. 'Where are the men who did this?'

It had taken some time to get all the cattle ashore and into the field. Now Rollo handed his uncle the binoculars, and pointed.

Sir George focused and turned the glasses on to the Blackscar Box. The tide, they say, comes in at the speed of a galloping horse. Now it had completely drowned the causeway, and the two men who had tried to run off the island had been caught fair and square.

Looking through the glasses, Sir George found himself staring at the terrified, grimacing faces of Dr Manners and the vet.

'I'll get them when they come ashore,' said Sir George gleefully. 'I won't save my bullets.'

But at that moment there was the noise of sirens and three police cars came roaring down the hill.

'Bother,' said Sir George. 'They'll want to arrest them, I suppose.' He shook his head sadly. 'I haven't shot anyone for years.'

Twenty-seven

The cattle were back in Clawstone Park. The drugs they had been given had worn off; the beasts roamed as they had always done. Rollo, during his last days before his parents' return, watched from the wall.

The fuss and the excitement had died down – the stories in the newspapers, the visits from the police – but not everything was quite the same. The smallest calf, the one the children had rescued from the operating table, no longer behaved in the way that the Wild White Cattle of Clawstone Park were supposed to behave. It had become tame and stood by the gate mooing for the children, and though Sir George did not approve of this, the calf became a pet and wandered in and out of the courtyard and up the stairs.

Nor were the ghosts completely the same. They had used up so much ectoplasmic force at Blackscar that they wanted to rest rather than haunt.

'We *will* haunt, of course; we'll do anything to help,' said Brenda. 'But I don't seem to be into strangling the way I was.'

But the real trouble was Ranulf. Ranulf in a way had been the leader of the ghosts, the one that spoke for them. Without the rat he became a slightly fatter ghost, and quieter.

'You're pleased, though, aren't you?' people would ask.

'Of course I'm pleased,' he would snap. 'What do you think?'

But he was very grumpy all the same – and of course the horror of Ranulf opening his shirt had been very much part of the haunting. When a ghost opens his shirt and shows people a rat gnawing his heart it is one thing. When he opens his shirt and shows them an ordinary chest with a few hairs on it, it is another.

Then there were The Feet. They had forced The Feet to come back with them, but they were damp all the time and no one doubted that it was tears rather than sweat that they were producing. Nor was there any chance that they would be much use on Open Days. Ned had put on the CD of eightsome reels, and one toe had twitched slightly but that was all.

'I could go back to making lavender bags,' said Aunt Emily, but Madlyn said quickly that she thought this would be bad for Aunt Emily's eyes and they would think of some other way of getting hold of money.

And then something quite unexpected happened.

An American who was on holiday in Great Britain stopped his car outside Clawstone and asked if it would be possible to look round. He was very interested in old buildings, he said, and though he knew it was not an Open Day he would be so pleased.

Because he had asked so nicely and seemed such a friendly man, Sir George agreed, and he asked the children if they would show him round.

The American liked the dungeon and the armoury and the banqueting hall – and then they showed him the museum, where he admired the sewing machine and the stuffed duck that had choked on a stickleback and the collection of Interesting Stones.

And then he stopped in front of the Hoggart.

'My, my!' he said. 'But that's amazing. That's extraordinary. *I'm* a Hoggart!'

The children looked at him, hoping he had not gone off his head. A Hoggart was a small brown thing with a few letters stamped on it. What's more, it had been found in Clawstone; there was no other Hoggart in the world. Cousin Howard had spent many hours in his library trying to find out about Hoggarts and he had found nothing.

But the man repeated what he had said.

'I'm a Hoggart. I'm Frederick Washington Hoggart. Here – look.'

And he took out his wallet and showed them his credit cards – rows and rows of them – and sure enough, he was a Hoggart. He was also in a very excited state.

'Could you please ask your great-uncle to let me see that thing? I'll handle it so carefully you wouldn't believe. Only I must see it. I must see those letters underneath.'

So they called Uncle George and he took the Hoggart from its stand and handed it to the American.

He looked at it for a long time. Then very slowly he turned it inside out, to reveal a few patches of matted hair.

'Oh my, my . . . I can't believe it – it's incredible,' he said, and there were tears in his eyes. 'This is the most amazing day of my life.'

He was so overcome that they had to find him a chair.

180

'See those letters,' he said when he had recovered himself. 'They are the name of my great-great-grandfather.'

And he told them about Josiah Frederick Hoggart, who had fought under George Washington in the American War of Independence.

'He was with him when they crossed the Delaware and overcame the British, and later he helped him with his business affairs. And of course Washington never forgot a friend and before he died he left instructions that Josiah should be invited to his funeral. It was a big honour, you can imagine – he was given a place right in front and needless to say he ordered a new wig. A special one made by the best craftsman in the state. It was powdered, of course; he wore it under his tricorne. And then when everyone swept off their hats because the coffin was coming past, Josiah swept off his wig as well!'

Mr Hoggart broke off, overcome again by emotion.

'Oh, the disgrace,' he went on. 'The embarrassment! He sent his slaves running after it but it was blown into the Potomac River and was washed away. It was a terrible blow to his family – the wig worn at the interment of George Washington lost and gone. It would have been our way of proving what an old family the Hoggarts are.'

He stopped and dabbed his eyes again.

'It's very small for a wig,' said Madlyn.

'Well, it's only part of it, of course – but it's enough to show that it's authentic. Oh, wait till I tell my wife – Clara's so proud of the Hoggart ancestry.' He broke off again, shaking his head. 'Only I don't understand – how could it possibly have got to Clawstone?'

Sir George had been listening carefully. 'Actually it was found in an old chest in our attic – and now I think of it, it was a sea-chest. My great-great-uncle was the captain of a frigate and he might well have sailed as far as the mouth of the Potomac. It's not impossible that one of his sailors picked it up.'

The American was still holding the Hoggart in his hands. It looked more than ever like part of a Pekinese that had fallen on hard times. Now he rose to his feet.

'Sir George, I know what this must mean to you. You must prize it above everything in your collection. But if you would sell it to me – I can't tell you what it would mean.'

Sir George was about to open his mouth and say that Mr Hoggart was welcome to the thing, it had no value for him But before he could do so, Madlyn had stepped heavily on his foot.

'How much would you give for it?' she asked.

'Would you take two?' asked the American. 'Two million, of course.'

'Pounds or dollars?' said Madlyn.

'Dollars. But, say, if that's not enough, how about two and a half? The money doesn't matter to me – I manufacture non-stick pans and you'd be amazed how many people need those. I could go up to three but I might have to call Clara—'

Sir George swallowed.

'Two and a half is enough,' he said, and found his hand pumped up and down by the blissful Mr Hoggart.

'Thank you, sir. Thank you. You've made me a very happy man. Oh, wait till I call Clara. We'll keep it under glass in the hall where everyone can see it.'

182

Sir George did not say so, but he too was a very happy man. The money, carefully invested, would see to the upkeep of the cattle for years and years and years.

Knowing that the ghosts could rest now and that Aunt Emily did not need to make lavender bags or bake scones was a great relief. Even so, it was difficult not to be sad when the time came to go home.

For Rollo the thought of returning to London was made easier because of something his parents had told him on the telephone.

His skink had become a father. There were five baby skinks; not eggs but proper skinks the size of little fingernails. There'd been a letter from the zoo.

'So I suppose I'm a sort of skink grandfather,' said Rollo.

'We'll be back at Christmas,' said Madlyn, standing close to Ned as they waited for the taxi to take them to the station.

'And at Easter,' said Rollo.

But they were back even sooner than that because they were invited to a funeral.

Twenty-eight

Funerals are often sad, but this one was not sad at all. It's true everybody cried, but the tears were happy ones and the loud sniffs that echoed through the little church at Blackscar sounded musical and right.

After all, it was not a funeral so much as a reunion.

Three months had passed since the Clawstone Cattle had walked to safety over the water and Dr Manners and Dr Fangster had been taken away by the police. But the banshees had been right when they said they had remembered something important about The Feet. Many years ago they had gone up to wail at the funeral of a wealthy grocer from Edinburgh who wanted to be buried near his mother's old home by the sea, and after the ceremony the verger had shown them the tomb of Hamish MacAllister, the Chieftain of the Blackscar MacAllisters.

Even then there was nothing left of the brave chief's name carved in the stone except the ISH part of Hamish, but the verger was interested in history and he had told them that when MacAllister had been taken for burial, no one could find his feet.

'It was after one of those messy border battles where they fought with cutlasses and broadswords and axes. One can't blame anyone,' said the verger. 'It must have been so difficult sorting everything out.'

And when the banshees had met The Feet in the

184

gravel pit something had tugged at their memories.

Even so, it took a long time to organize a proper funeral. The little church was seldom used now; they had to get special permission and the ceremony they planned was an unusual one – but nothing, in the end, could have been more moving and more beautiful.

The ghosts and the children sat in the front pew with The Feet resting between Madlyn and Sunita. No one had been silly and tried to decorate them with ribbons or polish their toenails. The Feet were what they had always been: strong and manly – and themselves.

Behind them sat Aunt Emily and Uncle George with Mr and Mrs Hamilton, the children's parents, who had come up from London, and next to them sat Mrs Grove with her brother, the warden, who was quite well again. It had taken the hospital a while to find that his stomach cramps were not due to appendicitis but to something he had eaten, and when Manners's crooks were exposed it was found that the lunch box he took to work had been tampered with. Major Hardbottock, the man who had made the ghosts famous, was there too – and one person they scarcely knew and had not at all expected to see: Lady Trembellow.

The rest of the church was given up to visitors and most of these were ghosts. The ghosts from the Thursday Gatherings had made their way to Blackscar: Fifi Fenwick, and the Admiral, and kind Mrs Lee-Perry, who had passed on now and become a phantom too, so that travelling was much easier . . . and Hal, Mr Smith's friend from the motorway who had first noticed the cattle going north.

185

And then the first sonorous peal on the organ resounded through the church – and Cousin Howard began to play. Because he was a scholar and a librarian he knew exactly what was right, and when the congregation rose to sing the first verse of the hymn he had chosen, they found themselves quite choked with tears, for he had found a hymn about The Feet. It was called 'Jerusalem' and it began:

> 'And did those feet in ancient time
> Walk upon England's mountains green?'

The service went without a hitch. The banshees wailed, Cousin Howard played a last resounding chord on the organ – and everybody gathered in the church porch to watch as The Feet, like a bride going to the altar, walked slowly towards the tomb of Chief MacAllister.

When they reached the gravestone, The Feet turned shyly, so that their toes faced back towards the church, and the heels lifted once and came down again in a last gesture of farewell.

But only the ghosts were with The Feet in that final moment of reunion. The human beings had gone back, knowing that what goes on when the veil of reality is torn aside is not something that ordinary mortals should try to understand.

So they waited quietly, sitting in the pews. And then, breaking the silence, they heard a deep, ecstatic and very Scottish roar of welcome from beneath the ground, and knew that the MacAllister was complete at last . . . and that The Feet whom they had loved so much were truly home.

After a funeral there is always something to eat. The banshees had arranged a splendid buffet lunch in a hotel further up the coast, and it was now that the children found out why Lady Trembellow was at Blackscar.

She had taken on Manners's Research Centre on the island and turned it into the Blackscar Animal Sanctuary.

'You see, I read about Dr Manners and I wanted to do something. He was the doctor who did all those operations on me and caused me so much misery, and I wanted to undo some of the harm he has done. I've always loved animals and I needed to do something useful with my life.'

She told them that they had managed to save the gorilla and were sending him back to Africa, and already people were sending a stream of tired donkeys and unwanted horses who would live out their days in peace along with the poor beasts that Manners had tried to tamper with.

'Of course, money is always short but people have been kind,' she said, and she looked meaningfully at the collecting box on the reception desk. But for Lord Trembellow things had not gone well at all.

For when the police started investigating the theft of the cattle, Trembellow had come under suspicion at once. It was his gravel pit that had been used for the scam, his wife had known Manners, he was known to have wanted to get rid of the cattle. Worst of all, money had been paid into his bank account by the thieves who had pretended to be vets from the ministry.

So they took Trembellow away for questioning

and charged him. As a matter of fact, though he was a greedy and ruthless man he knew nothing of Manners's plans. He had really believed that the vets came from the ministry and that the cattle were buried in his pit. Nor did he realize that Klappert's Disease did not exist and that the stolen cattle were perfectly healthy. But by the time he had hired lawyers to clear his name, and then more lawyers and better lawyers still, all his money was gone and he had to sell Trembellow Towers and all his businesses. Now he and Olive were living in a little grey house on a council estate.

'But Olive is so clever,' said Lady Trembellow. 'She has a row of jam jars and she puts all their spare coins in them and counts them every day. I'm sure they'll pull round.'

There was one other conversation which Madlyn and Rollo overheard. It was between their parents and Uncle George and Aunt Emily.

'The children looked so well when they came back,' said Mrs Hamilton, 'and they seem to be so fond of Clawstone. I wonder if we thanked you enough for having them.'

'Oh no! No!' cried Emily. 'It was lovely! They were such a help!'

Sir George in his gruff way said, 'I can't think why you bring them up in town. There's so much to do at Clawstone; you could both find work and there's a house in the village if you wanted to be independent.'

Ned had stopped eating. All three children were eavesdropping unashamedly.

'Well, I don't know. I suppose it might be possible. Perhaps,' said Mr Hamilton.

And his wife too said, 'Perhaps.'

'Perhaps' is a word that opens doors. Sitting in the back of the Bentley as they drove away from Blackscar, the children were utterly content.

They were spending the night at Clawstone before going back to London. Ned was going with them for a long weekend and as always the ghosts and the children spent their last hour in their favourite place on the wall, looking down at the graceful white beasts that they had saved.

'Poor king,' said Rollo. 'He never got his unicorns.' But actually, even if he had got them, the King of Barama would not have been able to pay for them, because the prospectors who had drilled for oil in his country had been so greedy that all the oil had been used up.

So the King had no money and when he became poor he found that all the people who had fawned on him and grovelled turned their backs – and he decided to abdicate and go and live in the mountains with his old nurse, the one who had told him the stories.

And as a matter of fact he was much happier than he had been before because he became stronger and healthier and had all the wild animals to watch – and after a while he forgot about getting hold of unicorns because he realized that unicorns belonged in people's minds, and in stories, where they can run wild and free forever.

'I suppose we ought to be getting back,' said Madlyn.

But before they could get down from the wall something absolutely extraordinary happened.

It was the sound they heard first; a faint scrabbling, a kind of rustle . . . The noise stopped and then came again, closer and louder.

They looked down at the ivy which covered the wall but they could see nothing. And then they glimpsed a faint wavering shape . . . a small *thing*, which appeared for a moment and then vanished into the tangle of leaves.

Everyone's heart now was beating faster. It couldn't be, of course. It was impossible. But the thing was climbing now, slowly, stopping to get its breath. It appeared, came closer, then disappeared again.

And then, with a sudden bound, it had reached the top of the wall. It had become almost transparent, and so thin that it was a miracle that it could move at all; the bones showed through its matted fur, the yellow eyes were filmed over with fatigue.

But it had made the journey. Somehow, unbelievably, the spectral creature had crossed the causeway from Blackscar and survived alone in the chapel for weeks on end, waiting, waiting . . . And then came the funeral and the rat, utterly spent, had crawled into the boot of Sir George's Bentley and fainted.

'For heaven's sake, man, make a run for it,' said Mr Smith. 'The creature's done for. You can get away.'

Ranulf de Torqueville threw him a look of contempt. Then, slowly and carefully, he worked loose the buttons on his front – and, with a flourish, he threw open his shirt.

And the rat forced his exhausted limbs into a last leap and landed on his chest.

For a moment, nobody spoke – what had happened was too solemn for words. Then the children said goodbye and slipped off the wall but the ghosts stayed where they were, inhaling the warm and healing breath of the cattle they had helped to save.

They were no longer afraid of being left or being lonely. For they understood that when something belongs to you it belongs, and that is all there is to it. And as surely as the rat belonged to Ranulf, and The Feet belonged to the MacAllister, so the children belonged to Clawstone – and would return.

Turn the page for an extract from

by exciting new storytelling talent
TOBY IBBOTSON

Based on an original idea by his mother, the late, great
EVA IBBOTSON

Percy

The next day when Daniel came home from school, his new neighbours had arrived. They were called Mr and Mrs Bosse-Lynch, and Daniel's Great-Aunt Joyce, who had been spying from her window all day, was very satisfied. They had the right sort of car, and the right sort of clothes, and Mr Bosse-Lynch had started trimming the hedge immediately. Then two ladies from the town had arrived to clean the house, and Great-Aunt Joyce had heard Mrs Bosse-Lynch telling them what to do before they had even got through the door.

That night, when Daniel had put his light out and lay in the darkness waiting for sleep, he heard something. At first he thought that it must be a pigeon under the slates. But it wasn't the right cooing and scratching noise that pigeons made. It seemed to be coming from the wall beside his bed. On the other side of the wall, he knew, was an attic room just like his in the house next door. The noise was more a snuffling or gulping kind of noise. He sat up and put his ear to the wall. Now he could hear quite clearly. He heard

3

stifled sobs, and sniffs. Someone was crying.

Daniel lay down again and tried to think. Perhaps Mrs Bosse-Lynch was secretly a very tragic person, with a horrible sad secret that she crept up to the attic and cried about at night. He hoped not, because he didn't want to feel sorry for someone whom horrid Great-Aunt Joyce approved of. But it was far more likely that they had a prisoner in the attic. They had kidnapped someone, probably a rich man's daughter, and sneaked her into the house. Soon they would cut off her ear and send it to the desperate parents. On the other hand, it could be a poor mad relation whom they didn't want anybody to know about. Daniel's friend Charlotte had read a book about someone like that. It was called *Jane Eyre* and was one of her absolute favourites.

Either way, Daniel had to make contact. He sat up again and knocked three times on the wall. The sniffling stopped.

'Hello, who's there?' he called. 'Do you need help?'

Still there was no sound. But then part of the wall slowly went soft and bulgy. The bulge got bigger, and separated itself from the wall. It was swirly and colourless, almost transparent. Then parts of it started taking shape, a hand appeared here, a leg there. The air in the room was suddenly icy cold, and in front of Daniel stood a small boy in a nightshirt, with golden curls and big weepy eyes.

'You are a ghost, aren't you?' said Daniel. 'I thought you were someone in trouble.'

'I am someone in trouble,' said the ghost, and huge ghostly tears started to roll down its cheeks. 'I am someone in terrible trouble.'

'I think I saw when you came,' said Daniel. 'You were in the removal van.'

'Yes, I was,' said the ghost. 'It wasn't a bus.' The tears rolled ever faster down its pale cheeks.

'Of course it wasn't a bus, it was a removal van.'

'But I thought it was,' gulped the ghost. 'And I don't know where I am and I don't know where Father and Mother are and—'

'Please try to stop crying,' said Daniel. 'And keep your voice down or you'll wake Great-Aunt Joyce.'

The ghost was obviously a young child, and seemed to be working himself into hysterics. 'If you calm down and tell me about it, I might be able to help.'

Daniel was secretly a bit disappointed. Ever since the arrival of the removal van he had been hoping for something really shockingly ghastly, perhaps a leering headless skeleton or a viciously grinning ghost murderer who dissolved his victims in acid. Anything really that would scare Great-Aunt Joyce to death, or at least make her flee from Markham Street and never return. But if she came up now and saw this weeping boy, she would probably just slap him and shoo him out.

However, even a small sad ghost is better than no ghost at all, and Daniel was a kind person and more than willing to sort out his problems if he could.

'You'd better tell me the whole story,' he said, and Perceval, for that was his name, came and sat on the bed and began.

Percy told his story with lots of pauses for miserable sniffing and cries of 'Oh, what am I to do?' and 'I shall be alone forever!', so it took him quite a long time.

Percy and his parents, Ronald and Iphigenia, had materialized in good time at the service station, where they had met up with Cousin Vera and the other ghosts and spectres who had applied for Mountwood School for Ghosts. There was quite a crowd milling about the parking bay where the bus was to pick them up. Some of them were old acquaintances, and they hung about, chatting, catching up on each other's news. After a while, when the bus still hadn't come, Percy had got bored and wandered off. There were lots of great big lorries standing silent and dark in the parking area. Percy glided among them, peeping in sometimes to look at the drivers snoring in their cabs. They had little beds with curtains, which reminded Percy of when he had been alive and his mother had read poetry to him before he went to sleep. His favourite one had started, 'Where the bee sucks there suck I.'

When Percy got back to the pick-up place, he saw a bus standing in the parking bay, revving its engine. There were no ghosts to be seen. He cried, 'Help, help, wait for me! Don't leave without me!' and threw himself through the side of the bus just as it drew away and rumbled off into the night.

'But it wasn't a bus,' said Percy sadly, looking with at Daniel with tragic eyes. 'The bus had already left.'

'Well, why didn't your parents wait for you? They must have been worried sick when you didn't show up.'

'I don't know, I don't know. I have been aba . . . adn . . .'

'Abandoned.'

'Y-y-yes. Like the Babes in the Wood.' Percy collapsed in hopeless weeping.

When he had recovered slightly Daniel said, 'I still don't see how you could mistake a removal van for a bus.'

'But I've never *been* on a bus. And it had words on the side like where we were going.'

'What do you mean?'

But Percy could speak no more. With a final wail

of 'Poor me! Oh, sad unhappy me!' he threw himself face down on the bed.

Daniel heard Great-Aunt Joyce's bedroom door opening, and her tread on the stair.

'That's done it,' he said.

'I'll disappear,' said Percy. 'I'm quite good at it.' And he started to fade, vanishing just as Great-Aunt Joyce appeared in the doorway.

Daniel turned on his bedside light. Great-Aunt Joyce was wearing a flannel dressing gown and tartan slippers, and her hair was in curlers. She looked very angry, and peered around the room.

'Really, Daniel, this is appalling. What on earth is going on? I must have silence after my pill. I shall be speaking to your father.'

'Oh, it's you, Great-Aunt Joyce. I was having a terrible nightmare.'

'Were you now?' said Great-Aunt Joyce suspiciously, and it seemed to Daniel that she stared intently at the exact spot where Percy had just vanished. 'A nightmare, was it? That's what comes of not chewing your food properly. Poor digestion.'

When she had gone, a small voice spoke from the empty bed.

'She doesn't seem very nice,' said Percy.

'She isn't. We'll have to be absolutely quiet now, Percy. We'll talk about this tomorrow.'

MONSTER MISSION

EVA IBBOTSON

*'We must kidnap some children,' announced Aunt Etta.
'Young, strong ones. It will be dangerous,
but it must be done.'*

Three children — Minette, Fabio and Lambert —
are stolen and taken away to a bizarre island, home
to mermaids, the strange and enormous boobrie
bird, selkies and the legendary kraken.
But soon the children find themselves in great
danger as the island is under siege from a wicked
man with plans to use these extraordinary creatures
to make money. Can the children
save themselves and their new friends?